LABYRINTH

BLAZE WARD

KNOTTED ROAD PRESS

Reviews
It's true. Reviews help. Even a short one, such as, "Loved it!" So please consider reviewing this book (and all of the ones you've read) on your favorite retailer site.

Never miss a release!
If you'd like to be notified of new releases, sign up for my newsletter.

http://www.blazeward.com/newsletter/

Buy More!
Did you know that you can buy directly from the Knotted Road Press website?

https://www.knottedroadpress.com/shop/

ONE

Dan perked up as the truck began to slow down. The hill they had been climbing had been steep and a little windy, but he'd still been half asleep, after the long drive out from Seattle.

The road ahead dead-ended at a wroughtiron gate that looked like it might hold out zombie hordes. The thing opened immediately when Stewey buzzed the house from the driver's seat, and they headed further up and around a curve to the house that was hidden beyond.

At the top, they went ahead and parked in a circular driveway, behind to two cars each worth more than Dan had made in the last three years. Stewey, too, technically, but Dan's partner had been born to money, to his everlasting shame, heir to a mining and timber fortune and the given name of Prescott Stuart Ogden IV, aka *Four*, when he really just wanted to be a redneck.

The house in front them him was the sort of thing that *Three*, Stewey's dad, might have owned. Perhaps as a summer palace, since it looked to be only about twelve thousand square feet of space, red-bricked, and three stories tall, done in an early-Gothic, middle-Roman mix that just barely worked.

Dan climbed out of the pickup and checked his look in the side mirror one last time before he turned to the house. Clean-shaven, half-Chinese kid from Idaho doing his damnedest hipster look in the big city. Straight, black hair just the perfect length to annoy the wrong people. Knit cap with rainbow stripes to celebrate Pride June as an ally.

The front door was already open when he and Stewey approached. Their old friend Kate, was standing next to the prospective buyers she represented, a white couple in their early forties. Former software geeks who had won the IPO lottery, cashed out, and ran away from Seattle, with one kid apparently at *Yu-Dub* these days and the other at *Wazzou*.

The locals in this valley probably hated everything there was to know about folks like this, up from Seattle with money, from coffee weirdness to evolving grocery shelves, except for what the property taxes on a place like this would do to improve their funding for roads and schools.

Stewey might have grown up in marble and gilt, but Dan still remembered an aluminum double-wide that never stayed warm enough in those cold, Idaho winters. Hadn't been that all long ago, either, just ten years since he'd gone off to become a Vandal.

Dan unzipped his blue rain shell as he approached, set his shoulders, and approached with a smile. Seattle was cooler than the mountains, but they were close enough to

East of the Mountains for everything to turn from green in the west to brown here.

"Dan Holt." He held out his hand to the man.

"Mike Grimsby," the man replied with a smile and gestured to the woman. "My wife, Alecia."

Dan shook her hand as well.

"So glad you were available," Kate said, pecking him on the cheek before doing the same to a badly-blushing Stewey. She gestured everyone inside. "Shall we?"

Dan wiped his feet and followed the other three into a foyer larger than his apartment, all marble and old, dark wood, with a crystal chandelier overhead and a mezzanine balcony. The sort of thing you could get if you hired really expensive architects and interior designers and told them they had a million dollars to impress visitors with the first room.

Yeah.

Apparently, the Grimsbys had made out *really* well, if they were buying this place. Although, there was a hint of staleness in the air. A dead smell. The kind that suggested the house had been empty for some time, and just cleaned in a perfunctory manner by a hired service. The kind that only came in monthly because nobody actually lived here.

Dan followed as they exited the big space by going under the stairs, through a heavy door that led into a hallway separating the dining room from the kitchen. He felt better, looking into the kitchen. He had feared one of those industrial places, straight out of a restaurant, like people were doing these days to keep up with the Jones.

This was the sort of place his mother might have cooked in, had they lived in a house. Old stove. Older microwave. An oversize wine chiller, off and empty. Lots of counter space and a small bar stuck out from the wall like a peninsula.

Homey.

"We can't wait to rip all that out and update it," Mr. Grimsby said, pointing into the kitchen. "Move the back wall out eight feet or so. Put in two bigger stoves and a walk-in fridge, so we can host parties."

Dan kept from snarling an obscenity at the man.

Barely.

He smiled instead. Their money spent just as well as anyone else. And would.

Kate nodded minutely at him and got everyone moving again, out the back door into a…what?

Dan had played soccer as a kid on a pitch smaller than this manicured back yard. You didn't mow a place like this, you bought a herd of goats and let them roam free, checking in with the shepherd every week or so when he made it back to the house for supplies.

Fruit trees. Hedges. A concrete patio in three distinct levels with marble slab benches and roses.

And over there.

"Is that…?" Stewey started to ask in a very compact voice.

Kate stopped walking and turned to face them abruptly.

Dan could see the whites of her eyes, but she was all smiles for the yuppies behind her. Still, even Stewey knew well enough to shut up at that point.

Over on the left, back under some enormously ancient trees. A cleared, round area with white gravel and black lines. It left a cold, dark spot in Dan's day, just looking at it.

"I thought you two could take a look," Kate said in a tight voice, chopped into individual syllables with a heavy cleaver. "The Grimsbys are all set to make an offer, and the bank will be thrilled to be rid of this place. The former owner died without heirs, so he left everything interesting to various museums and such. The county got the property itself and hired the bank to sell it off."

Dan pasted a brittle smile on his face and directed it at the two yuppies who were suddenly in *well over their heads*.

"We'd be happy to," he said in a voice of false *bonhomie*. "Why don't you folks head back inside and relax. We'll be a bit, and then come find you."

The Grimsbys nodded warily and went back inside under Kate's serene eyes, sheep being expertly woofed into place should they think to stray.

Dan zipped his rain shell back up. It felt like seventy degrees had suddenly become forty, just walking through the house. But that was all in his mind, right?

"Gosh," Stewey said, dripping with sarcasm. "I'm sure glad you convinced me to leave the guns at home."

"Not funny, Stew," Dan replied.

"Not laughing, Dan," Stewey fired back. "That's a meditation labyrinth. A freaking powerful one. I'm surprised those folks couldn't feel the power that thing contains. Kate sure could."

"She knows what to listen for," Dan murmured. "Real estate agents run into all sorts of old, weird magic. Your average corporate drone has no idea."

He took a few steps in that direction, and then shifted to his left and walked some more. Just listening.

There was power over there. A fuck-ton lot of it packed down into a very compact space. Maybe thirty yards across the outer ring, demarcated by a low wall that looked like cinder blocks faced on the inside with marble tile.

Stark, white gravel. Jet black lines in a set of circles, guiding the walker slowly around the entire surface of the flat maze. A space at the exact center maybe ten feet across marked with a design that the eye refused to bring into focus. Occasional pillars or obelisks around the outside, on that two-foot-tall wall.

The entrance to the maze itself was marked with two obelisk-shaped pillars about four feet tall, flat, with objects on top.

Dan drifted closer, but studiously concentrated on not falling into the siren song that wound itself up as he got nearer. Whoever had built this had bound the magic in such a way that it would be easy to fall into a meditative trance, even before you reached the entrance itself. Walking one this big might take nearly half an hour to complete, and you might never notice the passage of time.

And then?

Dan could feel Stewey close behind him, a presence like a breakwater.

"You're not going in there, are you, Dr. Holt?" Stewey inquired with a harsh tone.

"No, Dr. Ogden," Dan replied, just as brusque, turning to his partner, and friend. "I'm trying to get a feel for the center. It's not a demon-raising circle, but it is a portal of some sort."

They moved slowly closer, both listening with ears as well as souls.

"Stepping disk," Stewey said in an authoritative tone. He gestured to the pillars by the entrance. "On the left, a closed iron container I'm betting probably still contains rock salt. On the right, that's a silver bird bath that no pigeon would ever touch."

Dan nodded.

Who built a stepping disk with this much power behind it? It would transport you to a matching disk, but with that much power the other one could be anywhere on the planet.

Who went through?

Or worse, what would come through from the other side, assuming that thing didn't open in one of the more dangerous planes instead?

Dan ground his teeth and pushed himself to the right as he got close to the entrance to the maze.

Stewey seemed to be having an easier time of it, but he wasn't as sensitive to certain things. Oh, sure, give him an arcane device to build, or a summoning circle to lay down, and few people could do as precise a job. But Stewey's arcane nature was grounded in the physicality of the world.

Dan was the one really sensitive to the esoteric. He was the guy who could walk into a library of ten thousand tomes and immediately pick out the three with magical resonance immediately. Stewey would have to touch a hundred first, just because the power had bled into them over the years.

Dan reached into his left back pocket and pulled out the simple knife he always carried. Straight blade. Eight inches overall. Single-edged with a thick spine. Iron-steel handle. Small runes carved along the spine of the blade itself and filled with silver. It was more a tool than a weapon, although silver and iron made it dangerous to most fey or eldritch creatures.

Today, he just wanted it in his hand as a security blanket. Like Stewey would have been holding his old Colt Python loaded with silver bullets in one hand right now. Dan assumed Stewey had a pocket pistol anyway. Probably in his pocket right now, engulfed in one mitt, just in case.

Stewey was like that.

Sunlight peeking through the clouds glinted off something at the center. Near the center. Part of the innermost ring that contained the disk itself.

It was hard to study, even from the short distance of the outer wall. All of maybe forty feet.

Bronze.

Bronze?

Yes, bronze.

"Whatcha got?" Stewey asked.

Dan held up the hand with the knife. It seemed to slice through the foggy murk his brain kept insisting was there, in spite of his eyes.

"Bronze," Dan replied.

"On a stepping disk?"

Stewey's voice ended on a half-crack, up a bit.

"My thoughts, exactly," Dan replied. "Looks like the grounding elements of the circle."

"You'd need at least six for a circle that big," Stewey said in a serious voice.

And he would know.

"Times like this, a trained chipmunk would come in handy," Stewey opined vaguely.

It was an old joke. You never saw chipmunks in the wild. Only squirrels.

Chipmunks were much better ninjas.

"Yeah, but they won't license us," Dan retorted.

He studied the circle more closely, trying to concentrate over the music suddenly pounding at his temple. Music that was only there in his mind.

"I'm going to have to walk it," Dan said.

"You are completely, fucking, insane, Dr. Holt," Stewey replied in a calm, rational voice. "That thing will eat you."

"I have an idea," Dan said, holding up his blade. "The knife protects me, a little. You tie a bit of line to my wrist and tug at it occasionally. That ought to ground me enough. I can't walk straight across that much power, but I can force myself through the maze faster. Maybe I'll stay here. And you can pull me over if I lose it."

"Yup," Stewey observed blandly. "Crazier than a shithouse rat."

But he also pulled a small spool of parachute cord from an inner pocket of his denim jacket.

Dan knew people thought Stewey was pudgy, but that was all the stuff he had hidden in various pockets for emergencies. Line. Fishing gear. Spare ammunition. A can of spam.

A veritable smorgasbord of prizes, like a magician's top hat. Dan didn't ask about spare rabbits.

Instead, he held out his right hand and meditated while Stewey tied a loop around his wrist.

"We're set," his partner said in a grim tone, stuffing his other hand back into a pocket. Presumably, palming that spare pistol.

The music got louder as Dan approached the entrance. It was like being at one of Stewey's heavy metal concerts, a nearly solid experience that resonated as much off the inside of his skull as his sternum.

Dan resisted banging his head a few times. Stewey wouldn't get the joke, although he probably only heard the music at a level that allowed conversation.

On the left, Dan found rock salt, like Stewey had expected. The circle wanted him to cast a pinch into the air, but he forced himself to close the lid instead.

On the right, a silver birdbath, maybe a foot across and four inches deep. Polished clean, in spite of being out in the open. Not even leaf debris. Just cool water.

The circle wanted Dan to dip his hand in and flick water forward onto his path. Wanted that REALLY badly.

Dan forced his feet forward, marching to the beat of his hammering heart, rather than the slow, meditative pace he achieved when he did *tai chi*.

Speed was necessary today.

Something jerked hard on his hand, snapping his head around.

Dan blinked.

"What?"

"You're halfway and slowing down again," Stewey called across the vast gulf that separated them.

Halfway?

Dan looked down. The sun had moved far enough to be noticeable. He was clear on the far side of the circle and two rings in already.

Crap, this thing was powerful. Anyone without help would just get sucked right down into it. A dangerous tool, even for whatever mage had scribed it. Hopefully, that guy really was dead.

Dan made a note to go look up the previous owner. He was unaware of anyone this powerful, anywhere near Seattle. How had the man managed to hide himself from the other players in the industry?

He looked up and locked eyes with Stewey, nodding to the man.

Thank you.

Another fast step forward. Force the music out. Listen to your heart and your footsteps, crunching on the gravel with little puffs of white dust.

Stewey took to tugging randomly on the cord, once nearly jerking Dan off of his feet. But it also got him grounded again, when his mind wandered off onto strange paths invisible to everyone outside the walls that had sprung up.

More time passed, a battle between the power of the circle and the sudden tripping jerks from Stewey, playing him like a shark on a hook. Back and forth, but never quite reeling him in.

Just forcing him to fight it. And the music.

A hard tug. Sharp. Insistent.

Something thumped his shoulder as well.

Dan snapped around, knife up, ready to fight.

"You back?" Stewey called, holding up another rock.

Dan found the gray stone as his feet, marring the perfection of the white gravel.

The music insisted he pick it up and cast it clear. Dan stood back up instead.

"You cannot imagine power here," he called quietly.

"Yeah, I can," Stewey laughed harshly. "That was the third rock I've hit you with."

Third?

Dan saw the other two. Smaller. Darker. Blemishes that angered the circle.

Stewey tugged sharply on the line, dragging him to one side. The lines rose up like walls in his head.

Dan shook his head like a wet dog. Shook his whole body, like that would rid himself of the power floating around.

Something withdrew under the assault. Dan found himself able to center.

He took two sharp breaths and looked around. On impulse, he swung the silvered blade before him.

Something worked, as the fog thinned.

Two steps would take him to the entrance to the stepping disk, but Dan had no interest in opening a portal to an unknown place.

Instead, he knelt where he was and studied the bronze *thing* set into the ground nearby.

"Oh, crap," Dan yelled. "This one will be right up your alley, Stewey. You should have walked it."

"What is it?" his partner called back, looking all set to pull Dan completely off his feet at the slightest provocation, like a man catching swordfish.

"It looks like spade money," Dan shouted. "The turf here is hard packed. One bronze spade money, about four inches long."

"Like real stuff?" Stewey asked hesitantly. "Spring and Autumn Period? That spade money?"

"Hey," Dan looked back. "You're the expert on ancient China and their currency. You'll have to tell me when I get back over there."

"What are you planning, Dan?"

"It's not binding the circle," Dan said in a loud voice. "Focusing it, mostly. Grounding it. Since this is a stepping disk, it looks like the money acts as something of a false ley line. Someone ought to disable it."

"I don't figure the Grimsbys are going to want to keep this thing," Stewey said. "They strike me as swimming pool folks. What happens if we take all six?"

"Shit, I don't know, Stewey. You're the adept on that sort of thing."

"Right," the man replied, tugging absently at Dan's wrist. "One stops it from opening, unless you have a bull moose mage pushing really hard at either end. Taking the two at the inner entrance will stop even that. If you pull all six up, that probably destroys the whole maze. You think you can do that safely?"

Dan reached out with his blade to tap the four-inch bronze implement embedded in the hard ground. He got a spark of light between the two, but no serious jolt. Static electricity, mostly.

He pulled back his fist just enough to poke into soil instead. A steel blade would have failed, but the silver runes lit up as he sawed through the magical bindings holding the spade-shaped coin to the ground.

With a psychic pop, it came loose from the ground.

Around him, the music decreased. The whole world seemed to get a little darker.

Just how much power had that bastard bound here?

For a moment, Dan wondered if he would end up enchanting a whole new generation of pixies and such around here, just from all the raw magic that was going to bleed out as he killed the stepping disk.

Still, safer than leaving it around. And the chances of it all grounding at once and generating a unicorn were slim. Maybe a centaur if the wrong critters were close by. Probably just a whole passel of magical rabbits.

Dan made a mental note to sneak back in six months and check. A rabbit with a unicorn horn was among the rarest familiars in the world, but that's what he thought might happen.

Money, if you could convince it to come home with you.

And, hey, the eagles and owls around here would appreciate him relocating critters that could fight back.

Dan stood with a deep breath. Rather than do anything else, he threw the spade money as hard as he could in Stewey's general direction. It popped audibly as it passed the outer barrier wall.

He could have taken the other one at the entrance, but that would leave an openable portal in place as the maze failed. Way too risky.

Something might walk through, or worse, be pulled from the other side.

Nope, pull the next one to his right, even if he had to fight his way through the magical wall binding the maze.

The silvered blade helped. Dan could see investing some money in getting a bigger one. A proper sword. The kind a werewolf hunter he knew carried.

Stewey would know someone that would have the right connections. Or maybe this would the impetus for Stewey to finally start blacksmithing. He had only talked about doing it for ten years.

The second money failed faster than the first. Water flowing out of a broken dam now.

The third came out with hardly any effort. Four and five as well.

Dan knelt at the sixth.

It was now the anchoring stone for what was left of the maze. The circle didn't want to surrender this last hold. All the power of the ley line wanted to bind this key to the earth and hold it there until the rest could be repaired.

Some bastard really knew what he was doing, constructing this circle. Stewey would be in awe of the craftsmanship. Dan felt like a Goth about to sack Rome.

Still, he dug the blade into the ground. It was like going through ice, rather than turf. He withdrew the blade and stabbed again, a little to the right.

The icepick motion seemed to help. Little puffs of smoke emerged from the holes as he fought the ground for control. His blade grew warm in his hand, but Dan just switched hands and stabbed again.

Something broke.

A hurricane of wind spiraled out and upward, like an air elemental unleashed. It knocked Dan on his ass and sucked his hat right off his head into the sky.

And then stillness.

Calm.

"You are a crazy sumbitch," Stewey observed.

Dan turned as his partner stepped over the low retaining wall and began to approach, spooling the thin line around his hand.

Dan shook his head to clear out the cobwebs that had taken root.

"Yeah," he agreed, rising painfully to his feet with the last coin in his hand.

It was warm to the touch but cooling rapidly. The silver runes in his other hand were fading as well.

"It's safe?" Dan asked.

"That last boom blew everything everywhere," Stewey said as he arrived. "Not sure about safe, but nothing about this chunk of land is special, anymore. What do we tell the Grimsbys?"

"Lemme think," Dan said, watching Stewey unknot the cord from his wrist. "I'm gonna need coffee, and maybe lunch."

"Coming up."

They found Kate and the Grimsbys in the dining room. The yuppies looked bored, but Kate's eyes got big for a moment as Dan and Stewey came through the door. Stewey had vanished all six keys into one of those pockets.

"Everything okay?" Kate asked with false innocence.

"Absolutely," Dan lied. "But I might suggest that the

gravel be hauled off and disposed of, assuming you weren't planning to keep it."

"Oh, God, no," Mr. Grimsby said. "Looking forward to putting in a pool back there. Maybe a mancave as well. How should we clear the land? What's wrong with it?"

"That gravel has an odd taste to it," Dan lied some more. "Maybe a downwind sort of thing. I can recommend an outfit in Tri-cities that are experts at that sort of thing. I've used them before, and they work very cheap. They'll haul it all off for next to nothing."

"Even up here?" Mrs. Grimsby interjected.

"The government contracts them to do these things," Stewey stepped in with an authoritative voice. "Mostly, you're just covering them for gas and lunch. Kate will get you the information."

Everyone was on their feet at this point.

Dan followed the other three with Stewey behind him, as they trooped out the front door.

They saw the Grimsbys into their vehicle and out the gate.

"What the hell happened?" Kate asked. "I made sure they were facing in, so they didn't see whatever it was you did. I nearly peed my pants."

"Someone had a very powerful stepping disk put in, Kate," Stewey explained as he stepped close. "Dan had to walk it to get to the center, so he could take it apart. If you get the Koladny Brothers up here as soon as the deal closes, they can rip all the top off and sell it for a ton of money."

"Really?" she asked. "There's that much enchantment bound into it?"

"Yeah," Dan said. "I want to know where the other end is, but that's tomorrow. Right now, I need protein."

"That's on me," Kate said. "I'm getting an enormous fee for this one, from both sides. Four other potential buyers have backed out for reasons they didn't understand. That much magic in the backyard probably didn't help."

Dan nodded. He felt drained, like part of his soul had been pulled out of him when the power exploded.

Definitely have to come up here and look for magical rabbits next spring. Maybe bring a virgin along so he could talk to any unicorns that got created.

But the deeper mystery, the man who had been able to bind that much power here, that would be waiting. The man was dead, buried, and nobody else was coming along to step in, or they would have already.

But somewhere, the other half of that ley line was waiting.

Who would he find there?

And did he really want to know?

CHAPTER

TWO

INTERLUDE: KHULAN

She studied the building from a coffee shop located across the street, but Khulan didn't bother trying to probe any deeper than the stiff magical barrier erected carefully around the space.

Khulan knew she could simply annihilate the shield, but that would tell the man inside more than he needed to know right now. Similarly, she could open it up to penetrate, but there was no way to do that and not leave a mark that she had been here.

It wasn't that imperative that she get inside. At least not yet.

Local contacts had been able to provide her a little bit of background on a Seattle company called Holt & Ogden, LLC. Had she lived in the West, they might have even been the sort of folks she might recruit or at least hire, but they were innocents in the larger picture of things.

Still, those two men had stepped into something larger. She would need to investigate them closer. Perhaps ensure that they were not working for her ancient enemy, even accidentally.

Eventually, Khulan would find the way to destroy Koschei the Deathless.

And anyone who served him.

CHAPTER
THREE

Dan walked into the office to find Stewey already hard at work. But his partner was a morning person. Dan preferred to struggle out of bed around nine and eventually brunch.

Stewey was usually up before the dawn, even in the summer.

"You did actually sleep?" Dan asked as he moved to his side of the office, facing Stewey across the two desks pushed together and putting his steaming travel mug down as he checked the pile of mail that had been delivered over the weekend.

"Did," Stewey grunted. "Good drop biscuits and gravy this morning. Chicken fried steak. Even the bacon was good. Need to call and wake you up early sometime."

"Five Star is not my kind of café," Dan said. "Food's too heavy."

"Your loss." Stewey looked up and smiled.

Like every day, he wore that ancient Resistol cowboy

hat that he'd apparently inherited from one of his dad's mechanics. Brown felt, beat to hell.

Dan preferred a knit cap or a stylish hooligan on his head when he had to. Something impeccable.

But he hadn't wanted to be a redneck when he grew up, like Stewey had. Dan had too many of those folks in his extended family, even the ones that hadn't disowned him for being too weird of a kid.

After all, how many trailer park kids manage to get a PhD in history from the U of Idaho? Worse, he hadn't gone on to teach, but moved to Seattle, where he did strange things that those folks couldn't begin to explain to their other relatives.

Easier just being a black sheep.

Dan looked at the stuff across the desk.

Six bronze spade money. Looked like the ancient Chinese stuff that was Dr. Odgen's specialization in his own PhD, where Dan had studied late Roman and the Dark Ages.

Like Stewey, with a quiet specialization in Arcane Studies.

"Figure out what those are?" Dan asked.

"I have not," Stewey said in an authoritative voice at odds with the blue jeans, tan denim jacket, and old concert T-shirt. And cowboy hat. Dan assumed steel-toed boots under the desk but resisted looking. "These have an ancient feel that almost makes me think they pre-date the Zhou, the Spring and Autumn Period, and go back earlier."

"What's earlier?" Dan asked, leaning forward to study Stewey, as much as the cash.

"Classical historians will tell you Shang and then Xia, but nobody has ever proven the Xia actually exist," Stewey smiled. "The *Erlitou* culture was doing bronze work and represents a break from the *Longshan*."

Dan counted it as a victory that those words actually meant something to him, but only because of the amount of research he had had to do over the years. Being half-Chinese, he'd always been the one prospective customers assumed was the expert on Chinese history, rather than the crazy redneck.

"I hear a 'but' in your voice," Dan observed.

"These aren't inscribed with any ideograms I recognize," Stewey admitted. "Either ancient Chinese, even Oracle Bone script, or arcane. That always makes me nervous in this industry."

"We don't know all there is about magic, Stewey," Dan retorted.

"Yeah, but usually you can see where something comes from," his partner said. "This is completely different. No cultural matrix I'm aware of."

"Lemme see?" Dan asked.

Stewey picked one of them up and handed it across the double desk. Dan took it and leaned back, trying to focus his esoteric senses on the thing.

Bronze cash, like the ancient Chinese used to make, but he could see where he'd been wrong. It only looked like that because he hadn't really cared that much at the time. Getting it out of the ground and killing a rogue stepping disk had been more important.

Two inches wide, give or take. Five long. Bronze, but

so clean it might have been forged yesterday, except for the feel of great age it gave off as Dan listened.

Etched with symbols, but none he recognized.

And power. The thing felt twice as heavy as it should, even for bronze.

"I got no clue," Dan finally admitted.

"Thinking about calling the old man and asking him," Stewey said. "Figure he's on summer break, so he might be bored."

"And he might be in Berlin, doing research," Dan replied.

"Hey, he's seventy-five," Stewey smiled. "Eventually he's got to slow down."

"I doubt a warlock as powerful as him will slow down before he's a century old," Dan laughed. "Side effect of that much manna. Still, I'll give him a call."

"We could be there for dinner, if he's in Moscow," Stewey smiled.

Dan nodded and pulled out his phone.

Coleman Battersby, PhD in History. Professor Emeritus, University of Idaho. Occasional Warlock and teacher of new generations of them, quietly and on the side.

Like Dan Holt and Stewey Ogden.

The phone rang twice and clicked.

"My," their spry teacher said. "To what do I owe the pleasure of this call, young man?"

"We'd like you to consider a consult, Cole," Dan replied. "We've come across something that has us rather stumped and would like to engage your idle curiosity to good use."

"What have you two done now?" Cole laughed. Dan

heard him turn his head away from the phone. "It's Dan Holt dear."

"And Stewey," Dan said.

"And Stewey," Cole repeated, apparently talking to his wife, Iliana.

She wasn't a professor, but was probably almost as powerful a warlock as her husband was.

Quickly, Dan filled the man in on the mansion up in the Cascades. The unknown owner who had left behind a stepping disk of immense power. The act of breaking it. The coins themselves. Stewey's theories.

"Most intriguing, young man," Cole said. "I presume you'd like us to take a look at these bronzes?"

"Yes, sir," Dan replied. "We're a bit stumped, even Stewey. Do you have dinner plans? We could be in Moscow by mid-afternoon, and we got paid a lovely fee for this job."

"That would be excellent, Dan," Cole's voice smiled over the phone. "Could you send us some pictures of the cash, so we could start researching now? Iliana was about to go putter in the garden, but the possibility of having to spend a whole day in the library instead would probably get her heart racing. We'll see you then."

Dan laughed and clicked off. Cole Battersby looked sixty, but Iliana could pass for forty if she wanted to dye her hair, and fifty the rest of the time. Those two were never old farts just waiting to die, as there was still too much to learn.

And warlocks tended to live much longer, so they married other warlocks and had kids with long-lived genes. Both would probably quietly see one hundred and twenty, if they were careful, although usually elders like that disappeared and faked their own death much earlier.

The mundanes *knew* there was magic, but few of them understood anything about it. Or how it was done. Or who did it.

Even Cole had said he usually only found one promising student in his History of the Western World class every decade. Finding two the same year had been a bizarre stroke of luck, and Dan and Stewey had become business partners almost immediately.

"We good?" Stewey asked.

"Send him some pics of them, front and back," Dan replied. "Then I suppose you'll want to drive Bessie, won't you?"

"Better than your tiny, little Cooper," Stewey grinned and stood up.

"I get much better gas mileage," Dan observed.

"Yeah, but we're going to cattle country," Stewey preened.

Dan couldn't argue with that. Stewey would be surrounded by his people, sort of.

And hopefully they could solve the mystery of where these cash came from.

FOUR

Dan wasn't going to argue, since the truck was Stewey's baby.

They had made it successfully over the pass in that old, battered, '73 Ford pickup, badly-faded red and missing the left front fender.

Seriously. The man had rebuilt the engine once, then replaced the clutch three times, and would not replace a fender? And don't give me any of that shit about *feng shui*.

At least he had a lockbox under the passenger seat that Stewey had enchanted. Kept things like magical bronze cash largely undetectable as they drove. Not that he was expecting to run into anyone, but those things were powerful, and you never knew.

So, Dan kept his peace. Stewey was a pretty good driver, and the air outside wasn't going to be hot enough that they'd fry if the AC died, like it occasionally did.

Stop for gas, coffee, and the best pastries in the universe at Cle Elum. Cross the Gorge and take a hard right instead of staying on the interstate. Othello. Washtucna. Colfax before dropping down into Pullman and then crossing over into Idaho.

Wasn't the fastest way to do it, but one of the prettiest. Almost as nice as walking across the bridge from Clarkston into Lewiston, further south.

They drove in companionable silence past the university itself, site of so many hijinks that probably shouldn't be discussed until the statute of limitations ran out, to the Battersby's house on D Street.

The house was old but loved. Two stories and a big yard planted with a variety of herbs and stuff Iliana grew for her potions and such.

Everybody who did magic did it a little differently, depending on their strengths. Stewey was grounded in physicality, so he could make circles and enchant physical items as well as anyone Dan knew. Dan was more sensitive to the flows of power, seeing them as colors almost and able to work with them like flows of tides.

Cole Battersby was more like Stewey, building himself little items that he used to focus power when he needed to do things. Iliana's potions helped her establish little wards and ripples around her.

It wasn't like the movies, or bad television, where some punk could just wave his hands and hit somebody with a lightning bolt. A really powerful warlock might knock you on your ass, but Dan wasn't anywhere near that strong and didn't know many who were.

Stewey relied on a Colt Python with silver bullets. Hit just as hard as lead and did bad things to people with the right allergies.

They parked the beast on the street and climbed out.

Dan had a bag of goodies from Cle Elum for Cole and Iliana, who met them at the front door with smiles.

Cole was English in heritage. Brown hair finally turned gray. Brown eyes. Fair skin.

Iliana, on the other hand, was Russian aristocracy if you went back far enough, the granddaughter of a duke that had managed to get out just before the Revolution and eventually migrated all the way to America. Blond hair that was vaguely fading to gray. Piercing blue eyes. High cheek bones.

Inside, they settled in the living room, surrounded on every bit of wall with books. Dan and Stewey were on chairs, with Cole and Iliana on the couch.

"So what are these things that have brought you two all the way out here?" Cole asked.

Stewey handed the man a leather satchel marked with various protections, and Dan watched him unwrap it, placing the six artifacts on the coffee table. Dan wasn't surprised that the six went down in the same relative locations that they had had when binding the circle.

"And nobody has any clue who the homeowner really was?" Cole asked.

"A corporation had owned it for the last thirty years," Dan spoke up. "There were a number of donations to various museums and libraries when he died a year or so ago, but I haven't had a chance to track any of them down to see if they had enchantments, as opposed to just value."

"I will presume you'll find some," Cole said. "This disk had power, and you say that was the only thing left?"

"We didn't tear the joint apart," Stewey said. "The new owners will probably remodel the hell out of the place, so it is possible we'll get a call if they somehow find a door that leads into a pocket plane where the man might have stored other things, but I didn't smell anything when we were there."

"And if he knew he was dying finally, without students of any kind, he probably collapsed that as well," Cole observed.

"Then why leave the circle?" Dan asked.

They might be Cole and Iliana's peers, but he and Stewey had only gotten their PhDs as a cover for their magical studies a few years ago, and these two had been studying and practicing for fifty years.

"Maybe he had visitors regularly through it?" Iliana asked in turn. "Do we know if the death was natural? Perhaps an enemy snuck in and killed the man but didn't want most of the stuff? There could be any number of theories."

"What can you tell me about these?" Dan pointed at the bronzes.

"I agree with Stewey that they only resemble Spring and Autumn Period coins," Cole said. "But without doing a lot of work, I can't tell you where they come from. Most intriguing."

Iliana picked up the last one now, the one that had anchored the rest. She studied it closely enough that Dan could feel the quiet surge of magic as she did something beyond just opening her senses.

She sat the coin down and rose silently, walking to one of the bookshelves and pulling a tome out to crack open.

"You have something, dear?" Cole asked.

"Perhaps," she said absently, bringing the book back

and resting it on the coffee table, open to a pencil sketch of several arcane symbols Dan didn't recognize.

She rested the sixth coin on it, and Dan could see the resemblance now.

"Stewey, your theory about it perhaps being Erlitou is probably closer than you realized, but not far enough north," she smiled at the blushing redneck. She always had that affect on him when he showed off being smarter than he wanted to admit.

"Meaning?" Dan asked, picking the book up carefully and reading the spine.

Except it was in Cyrillic, which was one he didn't know.

"My grandmother brought exactly one thing with her, besides all her jewelry," Iliana said. "This book. There might have been a dozen copies of it in existence, back when she was a powerful warlock within Russia, more than a century ago. This might be the only copy remaining. These coins are a Bronze Age culture, yes, but I think they are Siberian, rather than Chinese."

"Is that good or bad?" Dan asked. "My exposure to folks from the Northeast is all the times they swept over Late Rome and most of Byzantium. And Stewey's is from a later period and further south, I'm guessing."

"I'll need to translate chunks of the book for you, Dan," she looked at him with serious eyes. "But it's probably worth me taking the rest of the summer and fully translating the book anyway, after that. It's not a slice of esoteric studies that many Americans or Chinese are all that familiar with, since those scholars keep largely to the depths of the forests and don't talk much to outsiders."

"Who don't?" Stewey asked.

"Followers of the Baba Yaga," she said.

"The?" Dan pressed, catching slight Iliana's emphasis. "She's not a goddess legend that modern warlocks like us invoke?"

"I haven't read this book in probably twenty years, Dan," she blushed. "But I seem to remember that she's an immortal being, and just flavored so many folk tales when the Europeans crossed the Urals and entered Siberia proper."

"She might still be around?" Stewey asked, surprised.

Dan could see the man's hand flex as he wanted to reach inside his jacket and just touch the butt of his pistol right now, but he refrained.

"After dinner, you two will stay here tonight in the spare bedrooms," Cole announced. "We'll dig into our library and see what all we can find. When do you need to be back in Seattle?"

"Technically, we should drive back tomorrow after lunch, because I've got a meeting with a new customer to investigate her genealogy on Wednesday morning," Dan said. "Easy money, because she's a cousin of another customer, and wants to determine what ancestors she should invoke for good luck."

He caught the benevolent smiles on Cole and Iliana's faces. Most warlocks hid themselves away in other jobs, like teaching history at a university somewhere while watching for promising students.

In ancient times, others had been scholars of the arcane for hire, or simple adventurers. Dan and Stewey were still scholars, but most of their clientele was Chinese, either newly-immigrated, or perhaps ABC, *American-born Chinese*, who tried to keep to the old ways.

Dan was the front, but he didn't mind. The half-Chinese kid from the trailer park had always been something of an outsider but had been smart enough and lucky enough to avoid being beaten up. Or maybe his gifts had given him enough of an edge, even before he learned how to use them effectively.

Stewey was the specialist, behind the scenes. Dan read enough Chinese, both classical and modern, to get by, and could speak Cantonese well enough and Mandarin passingly.

Stewey knew every dialect and could read everything anyone could hand him.

And no, Dan had no idea what he wanted to be when he grew up, but he knew that Cole wouldn't say anything. Just be available to former students working in the *other* field that had questions and strange needs.

That was part and parcel of the business of being a warlock, after all.

FIVE

Dan smiled. At least his Mandarin was getting better, a result of all the Northerners slipping out of the Peoples' Republic as the structure got more and more unstable. Most of the Southerners these days had managed to wrangle UK citizenship, or shift across the Commonwealth, with a huge cluster up north in Vancouver.

"*Lǐ nǚshì, wǒ huì liánxì,*" he greeted her, rising and offering his hand.

Mrs. Li rose as well and shook in the Western style, her other hand clutching a scroll Dan and Stewey manufactured for her to start filling in family details. It had just enough enchantment on it, like a light glaze, to show up if you had the right senses, and to maybe extend its life by a century.

Then Dan bowed to her in the traditional manner of a hired scholar greeting a wealthy patron. That threw her off-base even worse than shaking hands had, because he still probably knew the old Chinese cultural styles better than she did at this point.

Her husband, if he remembered the other chart correctly, had been a manager of a factory in the Nineties, when the Great Opening made its way past Shanghai and into the North. The Communists weren't supposed to turn themselves into billionaire oligarchs, but enough of them had.

The Party was starting to take exception, and an amazing number of folks had all decided to join their families in America as a result. Seattle had grown tremendously over the last generation, at least in that culture.

And they paid well for a Westerner who could understand their needs as they tried to get back in touch with life before Sun Yat Sen, and the old Chinese Empire he had overthrown more than a century ago.

They talked briefly, before she finally departed, mostly recovered from being flustered, and Dan sat back down and took off his *professional scholar* face. Grabbed his cooling coffee and decided that he was too tired even to try to focus on warming it back up.

Speaking Mandarin drained him. Caffeine only slightly helped.

Plus, something had touched him while he talked to the woman. Mrs. Li was a past-middle-aged Chinese woman, finally on the back side of that zone from thirty to sixty where they never seemed to age, just before they suddenly showed their years again. And she was utterly mundane.

In fact, he'd had to dive deep with her cousin, just to find any warlocks or beings of power in their combined ancestry.

It was almost like magic itself was slowly drying up in

the world. That made no sense, but the rightness of the thought grabbed him by the scruff of the neck and shook him inside, so Dan made a note to dig back into all those genealogical records and see if there was any truth to it.

Right now, however, he needed to make sure he was safe. Even in a city the size and complexity of Greater Seattle, there were only perhaps four dozen active warlocks of any power that he was aware of, with the assumption of at least that many again hiding for one reason or another.

Call it one hundred people with the talent and the training to enchant things and detect others. Warlocks of any power. Out of nearly four million people, when you added Pierce and Snohomish Counties to King. Throw in maybe five hundred or a thousand more with some shard of talent that had never been trained or wasn't all that powerful to begin with.

Something had touched him while he had been talking to Mrs. Li.

Just a brush. More a feather than a poke. Just trailed by and brushed against the shell of defensiveness he kept around him at all times. Wouldn't stop a bullet, or even a spell more powerful than a first-year student learned, but let him know when someone power nearby.

Stewey might have missed it, unless he had placed four enchanted coins on the table when he first sat down. Then one of them might have glowed, but his friend wouldn't have been that obvious in public.

Someone had recognized Dan for what they thought he was, and perhaps politely said hello. Or wondered if he would even notice.

Dan sipped some more coffee and looked around,

letting his senses expand as far as the walls in this coffee shop. Power was inversely proportional to distance on the square, so three times as far was nine times weaker, but he just wanted to reciprocate.

There. Not even looking at him, but she turned now and smiled in his direction.

What the hell. Dan was single. She was a petite blonde with high cheekbones. Cute.

And she smiled directly at him as he let his senses return to mostly normal.

He got up and grabbed his cup, walking slowly but deliberately in her direction, over into a corner booth she had to herself.

Dan stopped at about two paces away and smiled politely. Extended his senses again but focused them on her.

Got exactly as far as the little barrier she was holding and stopped, like mist on a windshield. Not even the little pop of a raindrop.

So, more powerful than he had expected. Way more powerful than him. Or Cole.

Top rate warlock of some sort. And completely unknown.

The woman cocked her head up at him. Dan felt her probe coming back.

He didn't try to parry it, unsure if he even could without turning this into full-bore combat, which was just about the dumbest thing you could do in a coffee shop.

It was almost impossible to hurt a mundane with magic. You had to open yourself to the power in the first place to be affected by it. But him stumbling backwards and tripping over a table was a sure way to send someone to the emergency clinic down the street.

And she didn't probe him hard.

Dan was reminded of the time he had met a date at her apartment and let her dog sniff him imperiously and expertly, before the little furball climbed up on the sofa and flopped into his lap for scritches. Dogs and horses had always been like that with Dan.

Dan indicated the booth silently.

"Join me," she offered in an accent that Dan couldn't place.

Dan sat, clear across the booth from her and right at the edge, so he could get up and walk away quickly if he needed to.

She had pretty green eyes. Blonde hair a little past her collar, thick and straight with a slight curl at the end. High cheekbones. Wide eyes.

Not Chinese, but not Russian like Iliana, either. Maybe a mix of the two.

Dan felt his stomach go ice cold.

Midway between Beijing and Moscow was Siberia.

Consciously, he set all his barriers harder now, not that it would do him any good if she was serious, but he had no idea what this woman wanted.

Maybe it was coincidence.

And maybe Stewey would buy a sports car tomorrow and start dressing in white linen suits, swapping his battered cowboy hat for a stylish Panama.

"Dan Holt," he said, feeling like a kid that had just been dragged kicking and screaming to the dentist. He didn't bother holding a hand out to shake.

Strangers in the industry didn't touch, as a rule. Too easy to do someone wrong.

"Khulan Zima," she replied, again with an accent that told him English was her eighth or maybe tenth language.

"I don't believe we've met," Dan nodded.

He would have remembered a woman this beautiful. Or a warlock with that much power at her fingertips. It was almost like being back home when he was a kid, watching the storm's hammerhead rise and start charging the air.

Right before the mushroom broke over and started to hammer the dust.

Rather than answer, she smiled at him. Dan had no idea how effective she'd been probing his defenses. Or how much she might have learned about him.

"Chance meeting?" Dan asked, hoping against all hope. "New in town and just happened into the shop?"

He'd been speaking English. She replied in a language he didn't understand. Guttural and clenched-jaw, so he supposed Russian.

Dan shook his head. If he was in a better mood, and not tired from dealing with Mrs. Li for an hour, he could probably cast a little something that would make her words understandable, but he was tired.

And she was a complete stranger whose behavior might be verging on rude.

Khulan smiled and switched to Mandarin instead. Her accent was still weird, but Dan could follow. Glancing around, they were mostly surrounded by Anglo hipsters, so the chances of anyone else in here following her words were pretty low.

"I'm following up on a mystery," she said.

At least that was what his brain wanted to translate it to. Several of the words and intonations had layers of meaning. Stewey could fence with her all day.

"I occasionally solve mysteries," Dan offered, still on edge, tired, and starting to get a little grumpy.

Cute or not, he felt like she was being a little brusque. Maybe that was just who she was.

"I sought you out," she said, face smiling even as those pretty, jade eyes got cold and hard.

He didn't think she was casting anything, and he couldn't feel any stir in the currents around him.

Stewey would have put a hand on a pistol right now, but he was like that when people got pushy. Part of the reason Dan did most of the client interactions. Angry customers don't refer their cousins.

Still, he could play rough, if he wanted to.

That even sounded nice about now, as well.

Dan unzipped his outside breast pocket where his phone was and pulled out a handmade business card holder he'd gotten as part of a Kickstarter project. Two thin plates of dark hickory wood, stained and polished, held together with an elastic strap in a matching brown.

He pulled a business card from the stack it held and slid it across the table to the woman.

"I keep normal business hours," he said with an equally frosty smile. "However, from here I have another meeting I need to keep, or I would love to chat more."

Rather than waiting for her to answer, Dan slid from the booth and rose. He bowed more deeply to the woman that he had to Mrs. Li, but that was appropriate for someone as powerful as she obviously was in the arts.

He paused when he got to the front door and looked back. Khulan Zima had not moved from her booth. She smiled at him and nodded more graciously than he had expected.

Dan walked out, letting her have this round.

He had no doubts he'd be seeing this woman again.

None whatsoever.

CHAPTER

SIX

Because libraries were considered sacred ground by pretty much everybody, most of them had some level of quiet enchantments added surreptitiously by the locals. Nothing powerful, but enough to remind everyone to behave when they walked in.

Dan had ended up at the Cap Hill Library, off Harvard at Republican. He needed some time to decompress from Mrs. Li and that stranger.

Khulan Zima.

Dan pulled out his phone and started typing as he sat. He possibly could have pinged Stewey but wasn't sure what the redneck could do at this point. She hadn't threatened him in any way, other than being powerful and female. He supposed a competent female was enough threat to most of the men he'd known, but they were fools.

This woman was just flat dangerous.

Khulan. Two obvious options, neither of which thrilled him.

A Mongolian word for an *Onager*, also called the Mongolian Wild Horse. Probably not.

The second wife of Temüjin, the man known to Westerners as Genghis Khan, Mongolian Warlord and founder of one of the greatest empires in history.

Mongolia wasn't that far from Siberia, culturally or physically.

That stepping disk had gone somewhere. Had he managed to piss off the folks at the other end by destroying it? Some might equate his actions with crude vandalism, but what moron left a disk that powerful just lying around?

The man who lived there should have either made arrangements for an heir to take possession of everything or dismantled it properly. Unless he'd died more suddenly than he had expected, but anyone powerful enough to have killed someone like that would have wanted to take possession of that power.

Unless it went someplace that person didn't want to go.

Dan was going to have to go deeper into the corporate shells that Kate had been dealing with. Maybe ask Gavin to see if he could find anything.

Dan didn't know anybody better at meandering down into the bowels of the internet and coming up with pearls than Gavin. Probably should have stopped into the man's bookstore yesterday, but you couldn't just pop in for five minutes. Not *Soviet Books* in Moscow, Idaho.

Gavin himself had exactly enough talent to be able to look at an old book and know if had any esoteric value or was just another wet dream about pyramid power written by some snake oil salesman. Or whatever the hipsters were deluding themselves with these days.

Dan added a note to another file to send Gavin an email later with some details and a request.

Last name Zima?

A Slavic name meaning *cold* or *winter*. Czech or possibly Russian. Either a nickname accorded someone with a gloomy or unapproachable personality, or who was from a particularly cold place.

Marvelous.

Dan opened his phone's map and backed it all the way out, then dove in on Irkutsk, near the southern end of… Lake Baikal? Lots of nothingness there as he trailed north. Very few roads. Endless space not particularly filled with people.

Shit.

Siberian runes. Angry Mongols. Powerful strangers about.

Just exactly what his Wednesday needed, right?

Dan took a deep breath and looked around. He knew what her aura tasted like but couldn't detect any scent of her in the building when he pushed outward. Not even old ones. Hopefully, she'd never been to Seattle before, so anyplace she went, she might leave a trace.

Still, this was a library. They ought to have something he could use.

Dan got up from the chair and headed to the computer to start looking for whatever they might have on Siberian culture. Iliana had promised him a quick cut on translation by Friday, rough but enough to get the gist while she started working her poetry on it.

Dan didn't want to wait that long.

He didn't think this Khulan babe would.

CHAPTER

SEVEN

Khulan watched the man leave the coffee shop like a rabbit trying to pretend he wasn't afraid of the leopard. She smiled and cataloged what she knew about him.

American of mixed Chinese and European ancestry, raised in Idaho. Trained by a loose clan of magic-workers centered on the University of Idaho.

She had never had a reason to even travel as far as the United States, but Khulan thought a side trip might be useful, if only to judge the man's mentor.

Dan Holt hadn't cowered before her, even after she made it clear that his power and training was a fraction of hers. But he was also only human. At the sensitive end as far as magical flows went, which suggested he would have far less power at affecting the physical world.

The man had eyes, rather than hands, as it were.

The partner, Ogden, must have been the one that established and maintained the wards around their office and the two apartments where the men lived. More powerful as an Enchanter than most but tied to Holt in emotional ways that didn't include romantically.

Holt had responded to her shell's natural beauty, that mix of Chinese and Russian that the best of Siberian included. Chinese bones. Russian hair. Jade eyes of the rarest type.

He had respected her power, but not feared it outright. Reacted to her as a woman as well as a magic-worker.

At the same time, she had smelled nothing of Koschei on the man when she probed him. No indication that he was in service to the Deathless.

Khulan smiled still as she rose made her way to the door, having given Holt time to make good his escape from her. Not that he could have, had she chosen to leave webs in his path, but again, he had not known who she was.

Or what.

That was troubling, only in that it marked how much of the ancient knowledge had been lost down the generations, as her war with Koschei ground on. How much magic had been lost as technology slowly won peoples' minds, and they turned away from the esoteric lore?

It had been the worst in the halls of Europe, as the so-called Enlightenment freed men's minds perhaps too much. In their quest to destroy the religious ignorance of the Western Church, they had also undone the ability to understand beauty.

China and Russia had held out longer, but the twentieth century had brought both low. Colonialism had done in much of the rest of the world, breaking them of the old ways as they sought to ape their masters. Those that weren't killed outright because of their power.

Even today, the level of available energy she could reach was so rare that Khulan had difficulties with some of the spells and incantations she knew. Things that had been simple in previous millennia.

She would need allies and knew very few on this continent.

But the war was coming here, again.

And Dan Holt had walked right into the middle of it.

CHAPTER

EIGHT

"Whatcha got?"

The voice caused Dan to jump halfway out of his chair.

Stewey, practicing *sneaky*, apparently.

Dan put the book down and tried to jump-start his heart.

"Oh, hey, sorry, man." Stewey looked chagrined.

Dan had returned to the office after the library, just because it had stronger barriers around it than his apartment did. It had ended up being a hell of a walk back from the library, even with the trolley, to get to the International District.

Time Dan had used to try to get his head on straighter, rather than riding the bus. The drizzle had held off long enough, and his usual messenger bag was waterproof anyway.

Dan had ended up on the couch where clients might sit if they got invited into the office, instead of a coffee shop or tearoom. Stewey dropped into his chair.

"You okay?" Stew asked carefully.

"Had the meeting with Mrs. Li," Dan said. "Something happened afterwards."

"What?"

Stewey was already reaching for his pistol.

"There was a woman in the coffee shop," Dan continued. "Petite blonde with Chinese features. Said she had come looking for me."

"Ex I don't know about?" Stewey grinned until he saw the look on his partner's face.

"If I rated me and you about a three for power, Iliana a four, and Cole about a five, I'd put her somewhere around eight," Dan observed.

"Fuck," was all Stewey had to say on the topic.

"Yeah."

"Looking for you?"

"For me, yes," Dan said. "Said her name was Khulan Zima."

"First name's Mongolian," Stewey said automatically. "Dunno on last."

"Internet says Slavic," Dan replied.

"Siberian woman?" Stewey leaned forward, staring intensely. "Golden skin lighter than north Chinese, but similar bones underneath? More Western eyes?"

"Yup." Dan breathed out slowly.

"What did she want?" Stewey asked.

"Dunno," Dan grinned. Or grimaced. Even he wasn't sure. "Left her my card and told her I had an appointment after that."

"So, we'll see her again?" Stewey's face got a hard, dangerous look to it.

"That's my guess," Dan offered. "Went to the library to decompress instead. And check out a book on Siberian culture and another on Russian folklore."

"Mrs. Li as difficult to deal with as her cousin?" Stewey grinned, taking some of the hard planes off his face and looking less fierce.

At least the man had never kept a beard or goatee long. The hair under the hat was getting thin, so that sort of look might make the man look desperate. Middle age coming too soon, kind of look.

"Worse," Dan let some of his own harshness bleed out. "Guessing we're looking at peasants, cooks, and house servants back a ways, once we get past the husband who got lucky and joined the party at the right moment in history."

Stewey nodded sagely. Those folks always wanted to believe that their ancestors had been great generals or scholars, not peons. Nobody usually wanted the truth.

Hell, even Dan didn't know, since Mom had been adopted out of a Chinese orphanage by a pair of well-meaning hippies, but Gran and Gramps had certainly given her a far better life here than she ever would have gotten over there.

"So now what?" Stewey asked.

"Seriously considering sleeping on the couch tonight, just because the enchantments here are stronger," Dan said in a tired voice. "Don't need high-powered Siberian babes coming after me."

"Babe?" Stewey's grin was back.

"Maybe twenty-five," Dan said, dredging up the nice parts about the encounter. "Long, blonde hair. Gorgeous face. Petite. Just a big block eight with a turbo sticking out of the hood."

He'd spent enough time around Stewey to frame some things in terms the man would understand.

"Well, she can't have meant you that much harm if she let you walk out of a coffee shop," Stewey offered. "Keep that in mind. But I can swing by your place and add some layers, if you think that would help."

"Maybe tomorrow," Dan said. "Serious about the couch tonight."

"Suit yourself," Stewey said. "I came by just to pick up the cash and stash them someplace better. Finally worked out a way to do a pocket safe that will make them invisible enough I don't think you can see them."

"How?" Dan put the book down now and leaned forward. "They bleed energy all over the place constantly, looking for that ley line I broke."

"Gonna turn it inside out." Stewey's smile could have lit the room. "Cole is always going on about the importance of ritual and flow, right?"

"Well, duh," Dan replied. "Arcane power doesn't work as well as it did before, so you have to rely on tried and proven methods. Everyone agrees on that."

"Maybe," Stewey said. "But I approached this like a redneck."

"I should be frightened?" Dan laughed.

"Maybe," Stewey laughed back. "But power is always the issue, right?"

"Right," Dan agreed carefully.

"So, what if I use those six cash to fuel an enchantment themselves?" Stewey asked. "I'm sitting on a battery that's already powerful. Why not tap that?"

"Safe?" Dan asked.

"You're the sensitive one, Dan," Stewey offered. "Let's see. Was going to call you anyway, but you're here."

After the rest of his day, Dan didn't have a lot of spoons left to argue, so he just shrugged. Stewey took that as in invitation to get silly.

Stew pulled a small, leather satchel out of one of the bigger pockets across his belly. Looked like the sort of thing an artist he had once dated had rolled all her pencils up in.

Stewey unrolled it and placed it flat on his desk. Dan rose and moved to the side, just for a better view.

From the bottom drawer, the redneck pulled out a fire-proof cash tray thing, a little bigger than a cigar box. All of the corners had been marked with various sigils, both protective and to conceal it. Inside, Stewey pulled out the bronze pieces one by one and put them into pockets on the leather wrap. He closed up the box and replaced it, closing the drawer.

"You can sense these, right?" Stewey asked.

Dan didn't need to open his third eye, but he did anyway. Hopefully it was just his imagination playing tricks on him, but he had the sense of great age and an endless depth of trees when he concentrated on them.

Dan nodded.

Stewey closed his eyes and moved his hands over the leather piece, not touching, but just brushing the air above them. A new set of sigils on the leather suddenly started to glow.

Nothing bright, but enough to nightlight a dark room.

Stewey opened his eyes and carefully rolled the leather up into the kind of burrito that you could get at most fast-food places if you went with the ultra-version. Stewey grabbed both ends, murmured something, and there was a slight pop of sound and energy.

"What about now?" Stewey looked up, his voice a little hoarse and ragged.

Dan opened himself to the cosmos. There wasn't a black spot where the leather had been, but it wasn't glowing in the slightest now. Just a mundane piece of cowhide sitting on the desk.

"Nope," Dan said. "What did you do?"

That was an impressive feat, given the strength of those things.

"Cole would probably call it a pinch," Stewey's voice started to come back to normal, although his breathing was a little heavier than usual. "I tapped the coins themselves to power the binding but layered them back onto themselves. None of the energy can get out right now."

"How long will it hold before the accumulation burns it out?" Dan asked.

One certain rule of magic was that you could contain power like that, but you had to build something durable enough to hold it, and even then it would leak. Swords and orbs had frequently been the receptacle of choice, historically. Back when the level of available power was supposedly so much greater.

Socrates had warned everyone about the *Good Old Days* being rosier in memory that practice.

"I'm guessing somewhere around a month." Stewey

rose now and slid the roll into a hard-sided briefcase he'd found at a pawn shop. The kind older than either of them. "This buys us time to see what to do with them and hides it well enough from a thief coming along. Will drop them in my safety deposit box on the way home. Dinner?"

"I'd be too tired and grumpy," Dan said. "Gonna walk down for some takeout, sit here to read, and then sleep. Come in quietly in the morning? I'll go down to the club for a shower."

"You got it," Stewey said, nodding.

Dan watched him depart and already felt better. The room was less oppressive, but he couldn't say if that was from the coins being removed from his range, or just them not being close.

He didn't like them. Would have already started making contacts about selling them to one of the folks he knew, but they were far more powerful than he or Stewey had realized when he had broken the binding and pulled down that stepping disk.

Enough to catch the attention of a Siberian warlock more powerful than anybody Dan had ever met? Idly, he wondered what she would offer for them, if they went up on an auction site.

Something like that was worth a whole lot of money to the right collector.

Keeping them out of the hands of an asshole might be difficult, though.

Who was Khulan Zima?

Or what?

NINE

Dan slept, eventually. Fitfully.

Dreams never quite ranged over into nightmares, but he surfaced time and again to disquiet.

Heart pounding.

Thoughts racing.

Demons pounding on the walls of the building to get inside, where they could feast on his flesh.

Dan looked at his phone for the time.

1:14.

Dead of night.

Why couldn't they call it something nicer? Death wasn't what he wanted to think about.

A sudden sound shot a bolt of ice down his spine.

Dan froze.

Someone had just tried to open the front door of the office.

All the shades were drawn. Lights were off, leaving the room in as much darkness as you could get with the streetlights bleeding around the edges of the blinds.

The door rattled again.

Stewey's enchantments pinged hard in response.

That was what had woken him. Something had hit them hard enough to break a hole in the magical barriers around the building.

Over in Leschi, Stewey had probably just levitated out of his bed with a pistol in one hand and landed clear across the room, looking to shoot an intruder.

Except the intruder wasn't at Stewey's apartment.

He was just outside the door from Dan.

Dan considered calling the cops, but he might have a faster response getting a pizza delivered. Too bad nobody allowed pizza delivery folks to carry swords in the real world.

Dan reached down on the floor next to his phone for his knife instead. The one he always had handy, usually in a back pocket if he wasn't wearing a shell. Usually, it was just a security blanket, but the tool was reasonably proof against fell and eldritch creatures.

Like whatever had just ripped a hole in Stewey's enchantments and was shaking the door in the frame right now. Your average homeless person wouldn't even understand why they had chosen not to approach that door, let alone sleep in the area. The magic would quietly convince them to move on.

Dan and Stewey couldn't solve the homeless problem around here, but they could protect their own building, and it helped the neighbors as well.

Dan rose, pulling the knife from the sheath and holding it with the two-fingered grip Stewey had originally learned from a tiny Philippino woman who understood blades.

The silvered runes along the spine were glowing when he did, but Dan had expected that. What was trying to come in wasn't human.

Dan had no idea what it might be, but there wasn't time to do much other than prepare a few spells he always kept handy.

Now would have been a nice time to be able to hurl lightning bolts, like they used to be able to do, if the ancient books were to be believed. Dan wasn't a bull moose sorcerer. Nor was Stewey.

Iliana probably was the best at that sort of thing, but it was rare, even among the warlocks.

Receding tides of time.

But the blade had been enchanted by Stewey, who happened to be among the best in the business when he could get off his ass and actually work, instead of reading ancient Chinese texts.

The silver glowed brighter as the door stopped rattling.

Dan watched the locks all turn in place with a sound like a bell being rung. One of the big ones that was down at the bass end of the keyboard. Mundanes might not hear it, but it was clear as the noonday sun to Dan.

He set his feet and pulled the knife back to his side like he had been taught, left hand out and open, ready to raise a shield, a magical blur that shifted reality in fuzzy ways.

Not enough to deflect a bullet. Maybe an arrow if you saw the whole flight. Pretty good in close combat, where centimeters counted.

The door flew open.

Dan's eyes were adjusted to the darkness of the room, but the thing in the doorway was pure shadow.

Man-sized. Man-shaped. Dan could see a pair of bright eyes in the head, but the rest was smoke cast solid.

As conjurings went, Dan was seriously impressed.

And utterly appalled.

He'd never known anybody that could summon a shadow servant larger than a rabbit. This thing was as big as he was.

It entered, popping with sound once as it forced the threshold barrier and was finally inside.

Dan felt the impact when the thing was finally able to see him.

Power.

Raw strength that could shatter diamonds, maybe, if someone wanted to.

The shadow servant took a step forward, long arms coming up almost like a gorilla that wanted a hug.

Dan pushed his blur into place between them. It was bigger than a traditional shield like a Viking might carry. Oval, but almost the size that his favorite Roman Legionaries had carried into battle.

A pilum right now might have gone over well, had Stewey silvered the tip with runes. So would a whole cohort of murderhoboes with silver blades, if he was wishing.

The shadow servant reached out and brushed a hand against the blur.

The air crackled with electricity and the creature finally emitted a sound. Almost a growl of surprise.

Dan stabbed with the knife, thinking mongoose thoughts. In. Out. Back. Quick.

Never make big swings with a blade. They leave you out of position and exposed to a counter.

He missed, and the servant pressed, sliding to its left to try to get around the blur.

The desks stopped it, but only because Stewey was more paranoid that whatever master had managed to raise a monster like this. The thing hit the wood and bounced, instead of just flowing though it like it had obviously planned.

On the desk, a set of sigils lit up angrily. Nothing that could stop a shadow servant from moving when it concentrated, but the surprise had been enough.

Dan hopped forward and bashed at the thing with his blur, again causing a spark of electricity that almost made him pee his pants. He poked at the shadow with the blade.

Contact.

It was like someone had suddenly encased his entire arm in a foot of ice. The runes on the knife were bright enough to read by, had they stopped for tea.

The creature reared back and howled, but Dan was sure the sound was only in his head.

Right arm numb, Dan tried to punch the thing in the face with the blur instead.

Contact.

Sparks. Left hand as hot as the right hand had gone cold.

More howls.

Dan got the impression of surprise, more than anything.

Sure, the damned thing was malevolence incarnate, but shadow servants were creatures from one of the outer planes given form and solidity by a powerful warlock. A conjurer's creature.

They were still dumb and cowardly if they ran into something they didn't understand. Like a guardian who had accidentally been asleep when they went to break in.

Dan punched with the blur again, trying to will his knife hand back awake from all the tingling of falling asleep.

Sparks arced.

The creature howled once and broke, fleeing for the door.

Dan charged after it in a fit of utter madness, trying to pop it on the ass with his blur one more time.

It managed to get through the doorway before he could reach it and then broke out through a gap it had torn in Stewey's barriers.

Dan slammed the door shut and collapsed to his knees, dropping the knife like it weighed as much as his car, and letting the blur fade. He breathed like a bellows charging a blacksmith's fire, gasping with effort.

Locks set, Dan turned and sat hard against the inside of the door, letting his ass keep things from opening it again, and letting the wood hold him upright.

Something trilled.

Again.

Phone.

Dan's phone.

He turned a deadbolt and crawled back to the couch.

Five feet felt like five marathons.

Stewey.

"Yeah?" Dan managed when he got it connected.

"You okay?" Stewey sounded like he was running. Then a truck door opening and closing. Bessie's engine turning over.

"Yeah," Dan managed between gasps. "Something just broke in, but I surprised the hell out of it and chased it off."

"Yeah, I noticed," Stewey said. "What was it?"

"Shadow servant," Dan said. "My size."

"No shit?"

"No shit," Dan continued. "Blur and the knife were more than anyone had warned it about. It panicked and fled. Where are you?"

"Blasting over the top of the hill and be there in five minutes," Stewey said. "You okay?"

"Numb, sore, and tired, depending," Dan said. "But it never actually touched me. Stabbed it once. That was a dumb idea."

"Yeah, one that big would be," Stewey ruminated. "Who the hell could send something like that? Your new girlfriend?"

"She's got the horsepower, but felt more like a Sorcerer than a Conjurer," Dan said. "Pretty sure I'll hear from her tomorrow, one way or the other."

"No way I can fix my enchantments tonight," Stewey said. In the background, Dan could hear that old Ford engine howling. "You likely to sleep again?"

"Maybe," Dan replied. "In July."

"Yup, about what I thought," Stewey said. "Let's get

you some food and caffeine. Tomorrow's already here and you'll need to power up to face it."

"See you in five," Dan said, hanging up and letting the phone pretty much just fall into his lap.

The room was dark again. Colder than he remembered, too. That shadow servant had been the kind they used to talk about in the ancient times, back when the Bible was being compiled, or when some of the Chinese Sages were getting themselves organized into schools of magic.

Nobody summoned things that big anymore.

Except someone had.

And if it wasn't Khulan, then there was someone else out there at least as powerful as she was.

What the hell had he and Stewey wandered in to?

TEN

Dan hadn't really argued the point. Stewey was Stewey, and he was driving. At this time of night, dropping down to First and running up north had gone pretty quickly, past the SAM and Pike Place, all the way up to Broad before doubling back up the hill to Denny.

Stewey even had the good parking karma tonight and found a spot just as a group of hipsters were pulling out to go home.

Five Star Diner. Home of the serious plate of chicken fried steak and fixings. Eggs Benedict and all the local variations. Coffee by the slice. Bad movies on the screen and a bar on the other side of the building for people not wasting calories on food.

At two on a Thursday morning, the crowds had gone home, leaving the place to the hardcore partiers. Stewey grabbed the table clear at the back, where a pay phone had once apparently resided, and sat himself with a good view of everything and his jacket unzipped.

Dan was facing in, but he didn't figure anybody was

going to sneak up on his friend. Even the waitress had a hard look on her face when she approached.

"All good?" she asked Stewey with the comradery of old acquaintance.

"Buddy nearly got mugged, down in the I.D.," Stewey said deliberately, referring to the International District on the south edge of downtown. "Gonna put some protein in him now so he can settle. Doubt anybody would bother us clear up here."

"Gus is working bar side tonight," she said. "I'll let him know."

"Thanks, Maddie," Stewey said.

Dan wasn't surprised that they knew Stewey in here. Or that he knew all of them. This was practically his other home. Would probably live closer, if he liked the hipsters and software nerds that were gentrifying the hell out of the neighborhood these days.

She left coffee. Dan supposed you could call it that. They had started with coffee beans, heat, and water.

Dan just didn't like coffee that charred. Not that he would complain tonight. The raw bitterness of his first sip jolted him enough to add more than the usual amount of honey and cream.

They had talked about it on the drive up here. Stewey had reset a few things, so at least he'd know if the creature came back, but nothing they had between them was tough enough, if someone could summon *that*.

"Figure it left a signature on the walls, both coming and going," Stewey said obliquely. "Come sunlight, I'll see what I can identify. Might be able to fashion a more personal seal for next time."

"You expecting a shadow servant next round?" Dan asked.

"As opposed to?"

"As opposed to his boss, maybe," Dan said, sipping.

Drinking, apparently. The mug was already three-quarters empty.

And Maddie had expected that. She was already at his elbow with more.

Dan made a note to actually drink this cup, rather than inhaling it.

They were alone again.

"We big enough to draw that sort of attention?" Stewey asked. "Can't think of anyone we've pissed off lately."

"I'm still betting on that house with the stepping disk," Dan said. "Nothing for the longest time, then we're suddenly neck deep in magical gators around here. Something was going on with that house or the man who owned it."

"So do we sell the bronze?" Stewey asked. "Melt it down and recast all that power into something else instead? Break them and bleed it out all over the place?"

"I don't need a unicorn roaming the Arboretum, thank you," Dan sniped.

He started to say something else when his phone chirped with a text message.

Wasn't a tone he had programmed, and apparently the Do Not Disturb function had been broken again. He hated buying new phones. You spent weeks getting everything turned on and off right.

Dan pulled it out and studied the message. Made no sense, so he opened it all the way.

That wasn't me. Khulan

Lovely.

The sourness must have been evident, or he was talking under his breath.

"Who?" Stewey asked carefully.

Dan turned the face around for him to read.

Stewey muttered several profanities under his breath.

Dan agreed.

Who, then? he typed back and hit send.

Why the hell not? She had his number from his business card. And had known something had happened, so she had at least one divination thread linked to him.

Dan was feeling grumpy.

Ignorance might be better. she replied.

Dan growled under his breath.

Maddie walked up at that moment, and they ordered.

Felt like a stupidly ugly day coming, so Dan matched Stewey with the chicken fried steak, eggs over easy, English muffin, and jojos. Slathered over with gravy and cheese. And gravy and cheese.

Bring it.

Who's trying to kill me? Dan sent.

Easier to explain in person.

Sure. Cap a perfect evening. Or ruin a perfectly good morning.

Whatever.

He showed Stewey the screen again, ranting quietly under his breath.

"Better than her showing up at our door in the morning," Stewey sighed. "Or waiting on yours when you get home."

That was the bitch of it. Stewey was right.

Only the awakened were at any serious risk of magic. Harming a mundane was almost impossible these days, although the ancient legends said otherwise.

You'd have to have something like a shadow servant handy, one who could affect the material world for you.

"Where are the cash?" Dan looked at his friend. "Right this moment."

"Under a rock in my back yard," his friend said. "In the box with my zombie bug-out kit."

So, the safest place Stewey could put something, on the off-chance that all those zombie movies and television shows were on to something and the world ended in a plague. The kind that only mostly killed you and left you hungry.

Dead of night. Zombies.

Could it get much worse?

But Dan didn't even think that too loud, afraid the gods and powers of the universe would see that as a challenge.

Join us for breakfast? Dan typed and sent.

Okay.

Then nothing. Like she didn't need to ask where they were.

Dan really didn't like *those* implications.

Was he about to invite the monster into his living room? Or the slayer?

ELEVEN

Khulan was still getting used to the modern world. Or rather, the chain of beings that she had bonded to stretched so far back that they still remembered the spread of iron technology that brought humanity up from the Bronze Age, a little over three thousand years ago.

Cellular communications were a novel thing, allowing her to remain in touch with everyone on the planet so blessed with such technology, rather than calling spirits to do her bidding and laboriously sending them to talk to others.

She could text a person via a modern device that was almost magical in nature, at least as far as most people were concerned. Fly on aircraft that could take her around the world in days, rather than months.

Travel from Krasnoyarsk to Seattle, although she had had to do that the hard way, since the disk she might have used had been disrupted by the very man she was visiting.

This was a modern city, with none of the hangover that had plagued her former acolyte. Khulan was just the latest to assume the mantle and could access all those memories.

Memories of Soviet Siberia under the commissars. The camps that were meant to punish people into forswearing the old ways. The terrible things that might happen to those unbelievers if they pushed too deep into her forests.

Farther back, to the arrival of the tsars, inheritors of the Golden Horde's power that had once stretched from the Pacific to the very gates of Europe.

Khulan drew strength from all her ancestors, bound up in her flesh, as she stepped through the door into an American diner.

She had chosen to dress as a Westerner for this. Blue jeans of the American style, even down to the labels. Inner shirt covered over with a looser flannel one, under a light jacket in black that wasn't leather, but had the waterproof nature.

Even her boots were American in style, mimicking Doc Martens to let her blend in better with the local populace.

Seattle was an international city. One of the hubs of the modern technology that had so undermined the old ways.

Her ways.

She had sat in a different restaurant earlier this evening and counted eleven different languages being spoken. It had brought a smile to her face.

Dan Holt sat at the back of the room, turned sideways to her in the row of tables opposite the heavy, wooden bar at which a few patrons drank alcoholic beverages.

Stewey Ogden sat across from Holt with his back set

exactly into the angle of the corner of the room, and his eyes roaming like hungry wolves.

He noticed her as soon as she entered. Perked up and muttered something to Holt. Slipped a hand into his pocket in such a manner than suggested the rumors of firearms were more than rumors.

Khulan kept both hands out of her pockets where they could be seen. She kept the smile on her face as she approached the two men. Ogden had given her the traditional top to bottom stare of a male seeing a beautiful female, and then done it a second time when he recognized a second magic-worker by the telltale signs.

The brooch on her shirt that looked to be simple silver in the form of a beautiful woman but anchored a spell to render her invisible to many Diviners. The necklace that would awaken if a summoned creature approached. The bracelets at her wrists that could expand to cover hands and forearms in battle.

Ogden's face grew serious, but he nodded to her, a mark of respect given to an elder of great power, although the man would have no idea how much elder she was.

Still, she nodded back, just as deep. Just as respectful.

It would help her cause to have these two men on her side, if not at it.

Not stumbling awkwardly into the middle of a war they had likely never heard of.

Holt looked up at her now, and Khulan could read the exhaustion on the man's face. The receding pain.

The utter determination that the only way he would be going down was by someone destroying him first.

Khulan couldn't remember the last time she had run into such stubbornness, outside of a mirror.

Or Koschei the Deathless himself.

That would be helpful, as well.

If she could reach the man.

"May I?" she asked in Cantonese, because that seemed to be the language both men knew the best, according to rumor, spy, and shadow.

"Please do." Ogden slid sideways enough to pull the second table close and indicated she should sit in the chair next to Holt.

Holt studied her from far closer than he had been earlier. She felt his senses expand and begin to wrap gently around her own barriers.

The man was a Diviner, just as Ogden was an Enchanter. Fully trained in the arts, but everyone had a specialization. A place their own gift was strongest.

Khulan Munkhtsetseg Zima had been chosen by the goddess because she was a powerful Sorcerer, even when young, in an age when great combat might be necessary.

When the War for Eternity might finally know an ending.

Now it only needed to know who would win.

"You had a visitor," she said simply, speaking to Holt but not excluding Ogden from the conversation. "A conjured creature."

"We call them shadow servants," Holt replied. "But I have never seen one so large. Or heard stories in recent generations."

"Describe it," she said, watching the man's mannerisms.

Holt gave her the details that she would have had to penetrate the office to gather. Plus, the man was a Diviner of some power and a great deal of potential, so he had the answers faster and easier.

Both men stared at her now, having finished their tale. Khulan had a smile on her face for the weirdness of the situation, and it was all the worse, talking Cantonese in an American restaurant to a man who was pure-blood northwest European, and the second who was half Cantonese himself, while she traveled under a Russian passport.

The modern age was truly an interesting place, even if her older memories were such much brighter with color.

"I believe the person who sent the shadow servant was Koschei," Khulan said simply. "Known as the Deathless One."

Holt perked up at that. Studied her closer, as if looking for something.

She stared back at him politely.

Allies, if she could. Making foes of these two would be stupid.

"I read part of a book this evening," Holt said to her slowly. "After you, I went to the library. There was a book on Russian folklore that mentioned Koschei the Immortal."

"Yes," Khulan agreed.

"He's not just a fairy tale?" Holt's eyes got a little bigger.

"If he is, then we all are, aren't we?" Khulan grinned lightly.

Probably not these two, not yet thirty years old, but

she had memories going back five thousand years, to her very first life.

"Who are you?" Holt asked breathlessly. "What are you?"

Ah, that was the better question, wasn't it?

The former was easier. Khulan Munkhtsetseg Zima. The *Eternal Flower of Winter*.

But *what* was she?

"Ancient," Khulan offered, not wishing to give these two men too much information. That might drive them away, where they would be easy prey for Koschei and his followers.

"Little help here?" Ogden spoke up.

Not much. Just enough to break the spell that had her and Holt staring at each other.

"Russian fables, Stewey," Holt said. "The man is supposedly immortal, because he hides his soul inside something, then hides that, then hides that. Like putting his soul inside an egg, and the egg is in a goose, and the goose is in a basket. Et cetera. She claims he exists."

"He's bound his soul to an item to achieve immortality?" Ogden asked.

Khulan was surprised, but then she remembered that the man was an Enchanter. He already thought of things that way.

"Wouldn't it make more sense to bind it back to your flesh?" the man continued. "Or does that render it vulnerable to a foe who can manage to kill the body and cut it out fast enough."

Yes, far more perceptive than his relative youth would have suggested.

"It does," Khulan agreed. "You cannot kill the body while the soul is bound elsewhere. But if you can find his soul, you can command him. Or possibly destroy him."

"And nobody has in how long?" Holt asked.

"Thousands of years," Khulan said.

Before anyone else could speak, the waitress approached. She moved carefully, like part of a choreographed dance. A glance back over a shoulder at a large male near the edge of the bar, with a hand out of sight, presumably touching a weapon.

Khulan didn't reach out with her own spells to confirm. She had studied humanity for enough lifetimes to understand the signs. Ogden and Holt were well-regarded regulars here, and she was a stranger at a time when Holt showed distress and Ogden showed a carefully-contained rage.

Khulan smiled up at the woman. Euro-descent. Possibly Hungarian from the bones in her face.

She switched back to English.

"Do you have green tea available?" she asked politely.

She was on foreign ground here. Better to be nice than cause trouble.

There was enough trouble coming.

"Sort of," the woman said. "Caf or de-caf?"

"De-caf, if possible," Khulan decided.

She had her own potions and spells that could keep her active, if she needed, without the addition of industri-ally-produced tea to disrupt things.

If she was going to spend any amount of time in this city, she would need to locate a proper tea house of the old school. Even if Seattle was known for coffee.

Khulan caught the nod from Ogden, indicating that everything was good. Both the waitress and the bartender relaxed. Khulan did as well. Summoning aid inside this diner would cause irreparable harm to the situation.

"Are you the goddess, or merely an acolyte?" Holt asked after the waitress left, staring at her from close enough that she could have kissed him, had she wanted to completely derail the man.

The mind might be ancient, but the body was still almost the same age as Holt, and she had been known by the other students as something of a goof, despite the power she had shown.

Still, it was a prescient question. Holt was more sensitive than he appeared. Probably smarter, too, although she already understood that both of these men ran deeper than she had initially expected.

The Westerners called themselves *Warlocks*, after an archaic term that mean *Oath-breaker*. Presumably the oaths of the Christian churches that had been dominant for so long and killed so many of her kind.

Holt and Ogden were both fully trained, according to the standards the West used. Powerful and competent.

But still human. Well out of their depth dealing with creatures that had not been human in thousands of years.

Khulan studied Holt closer. She cast a small spell and let him see it coming. Pressed against his defensive barriers politely with a Knowing. He resisted instinctively, but then stepped back inside himself.

It was as if he had met her at the front door and opened it for her to enter.

Khulan stepped into the living room of his mind. Into his soul.

She planted an *eternal flower of winter* in a pot by the window and watched him study it.

"Wow," he finally whispered after a moment.

Khulan broke the spell and was back in her own body as the waitress returned with a shiny steel pot, a mug, and a selection of commercial teas to pick from. She also brought plates of food, heavy with grease and salt for the two men.

Khulan's stomach nearly rebelled at the smell, but she understood that Americans had a vastly different understanding of *healthy eating* than she did. Plus, she didn't know any all-night dim sum places in town.

"Were you wanting to order food?" the waitress asked.

Khulan had forgotten about the menu, but she also wasn't hungry.

"No, thank you," she said, and the woman left them alone.

It was instructive, watching the men eat. Ogden nearly emptied bottle of red pepper sauce over everything, while Holt merely added a few drops.

Both men ate like the event was timed. Or perhaps there was a bomb just outside the door.

Perhaps an assassin, but they would be safe while she was handy.

But then they would need to discuss the future.

If these two men wanted to survive it.

TWELVE

Stewey studied the woman while he ate, keeping a small spell handy mostly as a tripwire, in case she did anything to his or Dan's food.

Wouldn't put it past her, but he didn't *Know* her. Hadn't had the woman reach inside and touch him, like she obviously had Dan.

No way of telling how much trouble she was.

Still, none of his items registered anything out of the ordinary. Not even whoever had sent that shadow, assuming it wasn't the creature across from him.

She might look human, but Stewey wasn't fooled. Top notch power. Seriously badass. Made Cole and Iliana look junior varsity by comparison, and him and Dan third graders.

Food was good. Miguel must have pulled a late shift. Usually he had the morning rush, and Walt wasn't as sharp on gravy. This was almost as good as breakfast rush, had he gotten here in another couple of hours. Maybe Miguel just came in early.

The woman watched him watch her, an enigmatic smile on her face. Probably recognized the charm he'd etched outside the door to keep trouble walking on down the sidewalk instead of stepping inside the café.

Wouldn't keep out things like her, but the really crazy homeless usually minded their manners better when they came in. Neighborhood was gentrifying hard these days, though. Pretty soon, just pretty boys and girls who worked in software would be able to live around here.

Fewer drug deals on the streets would be an improvement, but the old city was slowly drying up and blowing away. Just ask the old farts who had been coming here to eat since before he was born.

Dan ate slower, but he always did. Would eat less of it, though, like normal, so they'd finish about the same time. Stewey took a drink of coffee and pushed a spell out the front door, just in case someone sent another shadow servant after them. She watched with a tiny smile. Probably had already done the same thing.

His wouldn't slow something down much, but might give him an extra second to draw the revolver, and he'd loaded the thing with rock salt and silver dust tonight, tiny shotgun shells instead of bullets. Sting a person like a bee. Thump a spirit right upside the head.

This woman might not even notice, whatever the hell she was.

"So how do we know Koschei did it and not you?" Stewey went right ahead and asked.

Dan would be more polite about it. More circular. Stewey didn't have anything invested in the woman.

She turned serious for a moment. Probably thinking

up a pretty good story to spin for them. Like he'd buy anything this woman was selling.

It would all turn out to be rope.

"The disk would have taken you into my backyard," she said. "At least metaphorically. Why did you destroy it?"

"Someone died and left it lying around where any fool with a touch of power might have accidentally triggered it," Stewey replied harshly. "Folks buying the place were as mundane as bricks, but that would have just meant that they would have probably hired a team of contractors to rip it out with a backhoe. I can only imagine what would have happened then."

Stewey did appreciate the shudder that ran through her involuntarily. Made her almost look human.

He still wasn't fooled though. Oh, total babe, sure. Blonde hair. Green eyes. Teeny but well-built. Dangerous in so many dimensions he didn't bother classifying them all.

Warlock so powerful Stewey figured he'd have to go back to some of the ancient records to find a match.

He didn't think there were true immortals, but she claimed to know one, and Stewey suspected she was one herself.

"That's why we broke it softly," Stewey continued when she looked at him again. "Sure as hell weren't about to walk it open. No clue what might have come through. Or where we'd have landed."

"You'd have met me, quickly," she said soberly. "But nobody had told us that Faucher was dead."

"That the guy that lived there?" Stewey asked, noting

that Dan was still shoveling and chewing, but listening. "Been dead for a couple of years, according to the agent handling the sale."

Her eyes got a faraway look to them. Like she was about to ask him what was a decade to a being millennia old. Old farts were always like that.

Long, damned time to a twenty-eight-year-old warlock, lady.

Maybe she read his intent. She smiled.

"We'll need to do better, next time," she said simply.

"Next time you do what?" Stewey went ahead and asked.

This didn't feel like just dropping a new disk somewhere. Worse, maybe she was so damned powerful that it was.

Stewey had done the math out of sheer cussedness. Would probably take him most of a year working at it full tome to purify that much gravel and the stones that held the outer ring if he wanted to do something so stupid. The Kolodny Brothers were going to scrape it all up and sell it off to warlocks needing material components for stuff. Not much magic in the gravel, but damned pure, the way they'd handle it. Would hold another enchantment really easy if someone needed that sort of thing.

No, the power had been lodged in those six coins. The ones that would have taken him about a year apiece to form. And he was faster than anybody he knew at that sort of thing.

She studied him closer. He could feel the spell she sent across the table. Nothing powerful. Mostly poking for information. Wouldn't get much that way, with the things he had stashed in pockets to block that crap. Maybe she already knew that.

"That disk existed to facilitate communications and travel between the two continents," she explained.

Duh, lady. Easy way to walk without leaving passport traces. Where else does it go?

"And?"

Stewey was feeling his oats this morning, cute babe warlock or not.

"There are others," she replied. "Just not as directly, obviously."

"Know where you can get a really good deal on a bunch of gravel and stone, if yer figuring to build you a new one," Stewey said, maybe with a touch of sarcastic menace.

If she was that old, she was probably rich enough to afford it. Might teach her to pay closer attention to her toys next time and not leave a loaded firearm where a toddler warlock might get hurt because they didn't know any better.

"The Kolodny Brothers, yes," she nodded. "My connections suggested that they had been contacted to remove the load, as soon as the house sale closed."

"Is there anything else in the house that needs to be removed or closed?" Dan spoke up now.

Stewey hadn't felt anything when they were there, but he also hadn't walked every room with an orb that had been enchanted to glow in the presence of bound magic. Why the hell would you, if the place has been stripped to the walls already?

"I don't know," the woman replied.

Stewey grunted, mostly in surprise. Most warlocks were never willing to actually admit any sort of shortcoming. Too stubborn and arrogant. Always wanted to sound like a damned Sphinx instead, blathering nonsense and hoping you didn't notice the hand-waving and fancy footwork when they ran out of knowledge.

"How soon will the new owners take possession?" she asked, turning to look at both of them.

"Usually, thirty days," Dan replied. He was the one who dealt with Kate and her real estate needs. "I can ask Kate in a few hours and get an exact date. Would your friend, or acolyte, or whatever he was have left things in disarray?"

"Associate," she corrected Dan.

Stewey heard her emphasis on the word in such a way that suggested *fellow traveler who was occasionally as asshole* in her tones.

Stewey figured he was close enough to done eating at this point. Everything but about half the potatoes and half the biscuit, if he ended up walking right now.

"Why should we trust you any farther than I could drop-kick you across the square, lady?" Stewey asked bluntly.

Dan could good-cop this one. That was usually his job anyway. Stewey knew he was too lazy to take all that time at boarding school learning manners and put it to use, most of the time.

At least her eyes had a flash of honest anger in them for a moment, before she suppressed it. Like nobody ever sassed the woman.

Good to know.

Stewey had a pretty good idea how powerful she was. Didn't mean nothin' in this town.

She considered her words. Looked around. Considered the interior of the Five Star and the other clientele. Ground her teeth just a little bit as Stewey watched.

"That is not a story for such a public venue," she finally said aloud. "I can hide us some, mostly because Koschei is not that great at divination, but his servant will search for you and the bronze."

Just to be an ass, and to see if the woman would bite, Stewey tapped one of the pockets on his jacket like he had them wrapped up and on him for safe keeping.

Like a bloody amateur who was still wet behind the ears.

She blinked at him in surprise.

"You should have hidden them better," she said. "Unless you can stop a creature like that."

Stewey smiled enigmatically. Snub .38, hammerless and loaded with rock salt and silver dust, would do just exactly that. Might not kill the damned thing but would sure kick him in the balls pretty good if he came in here.

Dan knew the truth. Stewey felt him spin up a little something under the table, just in case the lady's greed got the better of her right now.

So Stewey was surprised as hell when the woman pulled a small piece of jewelry from her jacket and put it on the table between them. Watched her focus a SERIOUS amount of power in the item, so much that it glowed for just a moment, which was a really frightening to watch.

She looked at him with hard, emerald eyes.

"That should hide you from Koschei, at least for a time," she said. "And his servants, eldritch and physical. At some point, he will realize that you are hidden, and look for the shadow that it casts, and find you."

"Does that mean he just found you, as soon as you walk outside of range?" Stewey asked.

"He'll expect me to be here anyway," she said. "Faucher was an ally, but not a friend. An ancient who thwarted him from time to time, but not an immortal. Not like Koschei and me."

"So now what?" Stewey asked.

"You asked how you could trust me," she countered in a harder voice than she had before. "That will let you contact me, even as it hides you."

"And it lets you find us, lady," Stewey said.

"I would like to be an ally," she said.

"Are there secrets at the mansion yet to find?" Dan asked, kinda deflecting everything, like a good cop was supposed to do.

Maybe they'd played this game a time or two.

She shrugged. That much was honest. Maybe the first honesty from her. Time would tell.

"We can get you in, as long as you promise not to destroy the place," Dan said. "How powerful was Faucher?"

"Not as great a magic-worker as I am, nor Koschei," she said. "Better than either of you are."

Stewey watched her and saw the hesitation.

"At least so far."

"Then let's go look at the place," Stewey offered in a hard, smiling voice that caught the woman off guard.

"Now?" she asked.

"Truck's right down the street and fueled up," Stewey grinned at her. "About a three-hour drive from here, since we'll be doing it the old-fashioned way. Stop for donuts at Cle Elum and then we're in the neighborhood about the time it isn't rude to call our friend, Kate."

Lots of calculation in those eyes. One woman in a strange truck, in the middle of nowhere, with two men she barely knew. Sure, she could take both of them pretty easy, but she'd still be taking him and Dan as much on faith as they were supposed to take her.

He expected her to back out. Or need to call someone and check in several times, like any woman on a blind date with a relative stranger. Something.

Instead, she stared hard at him, like she was weighing his soul. Or his karma.

Did the same with Dan, maybe lingering a little longer.

"Okay," she said.

Damn it, he hated it when someone called his bluff.

CHAPTER

THIRTEEN

Khulan had ended up in the middle of the vehicle, mostly due to the size of her current body, tiny compared to the two males.

1973 CE Pickup truck. Manufactured in Detroit, Michigan, by the Ford Motor Company. Bright red at one point. Faded and touched with gray primer now.

One fender missing. Gone so long ago that the essence of the vehicle had changed.

Bench seat across the middle. Manual transmission controlled by a stick from the side of the steering wheel. The colloquial three-on-the-tree that older memories than her current body understood.

The machine had howled in barely contained rage, climbing over the pass that separated Washington State into cultures, but it ran with smoother power than a machine manufactured more than twenty years before Khulan was born should have.

The bakery had been as good as the two men had promised, a delight in smells and an array of options that was staggering, until she realized the relative poverty of modern Siberia, even for the acolyte of the goddess.

Khulan remembered her own childhood, those days before the goddess chose her.

The mountain road they had wound along was quiet at this time of morning, as the sun occasionally peeked out from gaps in the trees.

Ogden drove. Holt rode on her right. The need to shift gears and not have Ogden slam his fist into her knee, even accidentally, had Khulan pressed to her right, where she was violating Holt's personal space in ways that Americans were generally unused to.

It could not be helped. At least both men were polite, and Holt was rather attractive to look at, a good mix of European and southern Chinese in his features. She resisted the urge to flirt with the man, however innocent it might seem.

The situation was still utterly awkward.

She'd like to blame Ogden for that, but the man had called her bluff. Looked at her asking to be a friend and ally and challenged her to prove it by helping them with an investigation of the situation they had stumbled into.

Khulan would have done this more quietly herself, assuming that was possible.

Faucher dead should have undone most of the enchantments the man had created himself, knowing what an arrogant prick he could be. That would leave much weaker spectral defenses around the place, but nothing would be obvious, since these two men had gotten into the compound.

Unless Kai Damien Faucher had set up a trap exclusively for her. Probably her or Koschei, whoever arrived first to sniff at the ruins of the man's dreams. She would have to move carefully.

They rolled to the front gate, a wrought iron monstrosity that perfectly reflected Faucher's personal image. Holt had called the real estate agent who handled the transaction. Khulan had not been part of the conversation, but they had a code that would open the gate, as well as promises to let the person know if anything untoward happened.

Assuming that anyone survived one of Faucher's postmortem traps.

But Ogden was able to open the gate. The truck carried them up the hill to a plateau with a mansion that encompassed what a prick Faucher had been in real life.

Even the acolyte of the goddess lived in a house with only nine rooms. Faucher probably had wings of this building he hadn't visited since before Khulan's birth.

Ogden parked the vehicle and turned to her with a serious look on his face.

"This punk expecting you to try his defenses?" the man asked perceptively.

Khulan shrugged.

"He was an occasional ally," she said. "The War for Eternity has been going on for nearly five thousand years, and he was very much a late-comer."

"The what?" Holt asked just after opening the door on his side.

"War for Eternity, Mr. Holt," she repeated.

"Call me Dan," he said. "What does that mean?"

Khulan gestured for him to exit the vehicle and then followed. Ogden met them at the front of the hood.

"Koschei the Deathless seeks to live forever, so that he can own all the magic in the world," she said. "I and my predecessors have been fighting him for longer than you would imagine."

"Predecessors," Ogden said slowly, but it wasn't posed as a question. "What, exactly, are you, Khulan Zima?"

"Are you sure you'd rather *not* know, Ogden?" she turned to the shorter man, still a head taller, but broader and heavier than Dan.

"Stewey," he corrected her. "If you're going in there with us, I think we should be prepared. For whatever your buddy might throw at us. Excuse me, buddies. Plural."

Khulan didn't correct Stewey. He was as right as a mortal could be.

"I am two people, Stewey," she said carefully. "Khulan Zima was born twenty-six years ago, near Irkutsk in the Russian East."

"And the other one?" Dan asked. "The thing that took her body, in trade for power?"

Khulan couldn't tell if Dan was guessing or more perceptive than she had seen earlier. Neither of these men were what they appeared at first blush. She needed to remember that.

Both could turn into potent allies as their personal power grew.

Or terrible foes.

"An outsider would classify me as the Baba Yaga," she told Dan, waiting for the man to flinch or argue.

He surprised her by nodding.

"Iliana was right," he muttered instead.

"Who?" Khulan was shocked by the response.

"Our mentor is Cole Battersby," Dan said. "His wife is a Russian duchess whose family escaped the revolution a century ago and made it to the West. She has a book in Russian she's translating for me. I suspect you'll recognize much of it when she does."

Khulan felt her jaw drop open.

One of the old families has survived without her knowing? With the ancient lore? And brought it here?

A trip to meet the mentors would be next, assuming everything worked out here.

"I would like to meet them," she managed.

Dan and Stewey both grinned and set out for the vast porch. There was a lockbox on the door that Dan opened, revealing a key that opened the front door.

She grasped both men by a sleeve as it opened.

"A moment," she said carefully, studying the door frame.

Strange markings would look like an ornamental design to anyone without training or power. Neither Dan nor Stewey had triggered them, so Khulan wondered if they were tightly focused against certain targets or simply required a higher level of power to engage.

She already knew Kai Faucher was an asshole. How big of one was he?

Dan pulled a knife from his jacket and tapped it against the frame, eliciting sparks and causing runes in the spine to glow feebly.

"Stewey, this is up your alley," Dan said, stepping back and drawing her with him.

She ended up clear across the porch, standing perhaps a shade too close to Dan Holt. He had a pleasant smell, in spite of all the insanity he had been through in the last eight hours.

Stewey did not bring out a wand or athame to focus his will, which surprised her, as he was in the middle of the pack for human magic-workers. Then he laid his bare hands on the doorframe, and Khulan watched him push his will and a spell directly into the wood.

Impressive. Stewey had a gift for enchantment far beyond most she knew in this generation. Khulan made a note to see what artifacts the man made. With the loss of so much magic over the centuries—Koschei never to be sufficiently damned—fewer were born each generation with the ability to tap the remainder.

Perhaps shattering some of Faucher's remaining items would help.

Stewey turned to stare at her from across the distance.

"So there's four names inscribed here," he said. "Guessing one of them is you, because the whole thing's reactive right now. Should I break it, like we did the circle?"

"Can you do that?" Khulan asked, surprised. "Safely?"

"Easy," Stewey said. "This Faucher fellow had a penchant for false ley lines. No idea why he built here, except that he's way the hell away from everybody else."

"Are there any real lines around here?" she asked, reconsidering the entire situation.

"None," Stewey said. "Some down on the coastal plain. Some well inland, heading into Canada. Nothing around here, which might have made it quiet enough that he could hide. Nobody would think to look for him here."

"We're already coming back for unicorns in the spring, Stewey," Dan said, which made no sense to Khulan. "Go ahead and break it now. We'll just have to bring a virgin when we come."

That sounded like a story she would need to get from the men later. Right now, she heard Stewey grunt with effort, and the entire frame around the door lit up with blue fire, showing various runes that had been hidden.

The barrier failed like a burst balloon. Khulan had no way to capture all the power flowing towards her like a breeze. She could only hope that some of the locals had enough of the gift to make use of it, so that it didn't just flow back into the depths of the earth and disappear, like so much magic had when the people forgot.

Still, she held out her hand and pulled a handful of power to her. It would last her for a while and save her having to use her own.

"Okay." Stewey kind of slumped after the magical breeze failed. "Door's open. Probably the other three folks just got woken up from whatever they were doing, so we should move quickly."

Khulan agreed. She'd felt the pulse. Koschei would as well. She needed to ask Stewey who the others were, but that could wait.

The interior of the foyer was exactly what she would have expected Faucher to have. Dan led them up the over-wrought stairs to a hallway and then down the length to a double door that was closed.

Looking back, Khulan wondered if this hallway alone,

running along the spine of the second floor, had more square meters than her house did. A waste, doubly so when you considered how much power it would take to protect it from spells and summoned creatures.

Dan opened the door. Khulan followed him in. Stewey joined them.

The room was empty and immense. Indeed, the carpet had ended at the door and stone tile had been put here instead. Khulan had been in auditoriums that were smaller.

It took up the entire endcap of the building, with windows overlooking the front as well as the back and a view of trees out the side.

"This was his working library," Dan said simply.

Looking around, Khulan had to agree. The walls had absorbed a fair share of power over a long stretch of time, like the background radiation left three generations after Soviet weapons testing had moved underground.

The room smelled of stale magic. If that could be a thing. Bound up and gone sour.

How much power could someone pull out of the walls, if they could store it? How much would simply bleed away into the earth, some of it never to return?

"They will remodel this, won't they?" she asked Dan, referring to the new owners. "Lose it?"

"They will," Stewey agreed. "Again, maybe we can refer them to someone. Hell, maybe we need to get into the interior decorating business. Certainly, there's a *feng shui* element we could emphasize."

"The Grimsbys couldn't spell *feng shui*, Stewey," Dan said, turning to her. "What happens to all the power when they do? Better, if you're that old, where has it all gone to?"

She had hoped not to have this conversation with these two men. At least not yet. Perhaps later when they had built up some level of trust.

But then, how did you build trust except to give it?

"All magic wants to come to rest," Khulan said, echoing some of her earliest lessons as a prospect for the goddess. "It will flow into nature and the settle in the earth. Magic-workers, warlocks such as yourself, can make use of it. Bind it. Enchant it into items."

"Then where did it all go?" Dan asked again.

"Some of it has been bound up into powerful items that have been hidden," she said. "Much has been lost simply because there are fewer who believe in it, so they do not draw it from depths of the earth and spread it out, like watering flowers from a well."

"How much power does it take to keep a *Deathless Immortal* alive?" Stewey asked, studying her far closer than a man might stare at a pretty woman.

"I am not deathless, Stewey," she admitted carefully. "As each body ages, a new acolyte is chosen from a crop of new students. Often, a candidate might be known soon after birth. Khulan was such, and she chose to embrace the binding."

"You're talking in the third person," Dan said carefully.

They were speaking in English now. Had been since they left the restaurant in Seattle, although she wasn't sure when they fully transitioned.

"I have memories that are five thousand years old, Dan Holt," she said powerfully. "And I remember being offered the power of the goddess when I was still a child and the old acolyte was one hundred and forty years old. There is not an adequate vocabulary to describe being two people, except that Khulan is the person you see, and she remembers being hundreds of other women, stretching backwards in a chain millennia old."

"Do you miss being human?" Dan asked, with almost a mournful tone to his voice.

"Do you have any idea what it's like to be a goddess, Dan?" she countered, smiling with pure joy.

"So, you're not an immortal permanently stealing magical energy?" Stewey grunted.

"Not much more than you use, Stewey Ogden," Khulan turned to include the man in the conversation. "Faucher stole much more from the earth. I can sense that just from how much bleed is left in the walls here. Koschei seeks to bind it all, to keep himself alive forever, because each year it takes a little more to keep his flesh intact. That is why the Baba Yaga chose this form of immortality, originally. We are the memories and not the flesh."

"Weird," Dan acknowledged, but Khulan couldn't really argue the point with the man.

She had met truly magical creatures, things left over from earlier epochs of humanity, long before the rise of metallurgical technology. Dan might joke about meeting a unicorn, but Khulan could introduce him to several if he chose to travel to Russia someday.

She watched Dan come to some conclusion as he studied her. Unlike Stewey, he did see her as a beautiful woman. That much was obvious in his eyes, where Ogden's held challenge most of the time.

"All right, I don't know why that bastard wrapped a meditation maze around his stepping disk," Dan said. "Other than it would take someone half an hour to exit the labyrinth if they emerged at the center, so perhaps it gave him time to prepare defenses, since you say he was only occasionally an ally?"

"That's right," Khulan said. "Faucher was ancient and powerful, perhaps three hundred years old, but starting immortality today is much more difficult when there is so little power flowing free in the world. Even in America, which has not been so disrupted as Europe or Asia. He aided me when he chose and Koschei when the mood struck. But he was a private man at the best of times, so nobody knows much about him. Knew."

"And we're sure he's dead?" Dan asked. "The records only show that the resident was no longer among the living, and the corporation who owned the estate had put the building up for sale. Could this all be an enormous swindle?"

"Swindle?" Khulan asked, confused.

"If you change bodies every once in a while, could Faucher have gone down that same path?" Dan asked. "Fake his death, walk away, and inhabit a new body?"

Khulan felt her stomach grow cold. Anything was possible, especially if a man like Faucher finally confronted the death of his preserved flesh.

"Would it matter?" she asked.

"All interior furnishings were removed as part of the estate," Stewey spoke up now. "Many items were sent to museums, where us warlocks had an assumption that we might find some items of power hidden if we went looking. But if he's walking, he might have *sold* things off to someone else before he died and left many of the things here. Maybe he's walking around Seattle or Hong Kong right now just like you are, Khulan Zima."

That would be an ugly development, she decided. And she could see someone like Faucher doing that.

"And the power bound up here?" she asked, letting these men speculate.

They had been closer to the center of things longer. Perhaps they had better ideas about modern American culture.

"Someone breaks it when they buy the place," Dan said. "Proof positive to the rest of us that he's dead. Nobody would ever ask if he wasn't. Another warlock might come along and collect magical rabbits or pull some of it out of the air, like you did, Khulan. But his enemies would assume him gone. At least long enough for whatever revenge he had planned."

"How do we prove it, one way or the other?" she asked, turning from one man to the other, aware of how wound up both of them were.

Neither was focused on her right now, though, so she was not expecting an attack.

Dan Holt turned to an interior wall and walked close enough to lay his hands on it. Khulan felt the spell the man cast into the wall itself, the underlying ribs of the building pulsing back with power underneath the paint and plaster that had been added over the brick later.

"Stewey, there's something here," Dan said, drawing her and Ogden closer. "I felt it when we walked in, but the taint in the air mostly obscures it. He bound something to the wall here."

Khulan cast her own spell, but even with her greater overall power, she could not sense what Dan did. But she was a Sorcerer, not a Diviner like he was.

Stewey walked past her and touched the wall as well.

"Tastes like that damned maze the bastard left in the backyard," Stewey said. "What's behind here?"

"Bricks," Dan said. "This feels like it was part of an exterior wall at one point, with archways on the ground floor that have been covered over with wall. I can see how this was once the outside of the building when I look at it. Faucher, or someone, extended it and added this room where this used to be a patio."

Khulan wasn't an expert on architecture, so she had to take the man at his word. She stepped back and studied the entire wall though. Felt the falseness of it, like a mask worn at a ball she had once attended, over a space about three meters wide, next to the doorway itself.

"Stewey, there is section of wall that is fake," she saw it now.

Both hands up, she pushed some of the magic she had captured earlier into the wall and watched it light up with glyphs and runes.

"Son of a bitch," Stewey muttered. "Can you hold that?"

"Why?" she asked, focusing on her breathing.

The enchantments were heavy. It was like carrying one of these men on her back and trying to walk.

Stewey walked next to Dan and touched the wall in

three places with his right hand, palm flat and pushing his own magic into the wall.

It suddenly felt light, as if she had just set down a backpack full of schoolbooks to study.

"Dan, back up," Stewey said abruptly.

Both men did, moving next to her.

"Khulan, the outer wall is floating free right now," Stewey said. "Can you tilt it down and lay it flat on the floor?"

Could she what?

But the weight was lessened.

She tugged and felt the entire thing come towards her perhaps a decimeter.

Khulan concentrated and brought the top down slowly, focusing on keeping the entire thing whole as she did.

It rested with a hard puff of dust and magic that blew her hair back a little, revealing a stone wall that had been covered over before.

Khulan recognized the sigils where Stewey had touched it before.

There was a portal hidden here, where even the most aggressive remodel probably wouldn't reveal.

It was like the stepping disk she remembered from the backyard, but didn't lead to another disk.

Or rather, the one it led to wasn't on earth.

Faucher had hidden a portal to a demiplane, and nobody would have found it, probably until it was too late.

FOURTEEN

Dan's job was usually to run interference for Stewey. That had always been the thing that made them more powerful, more dangerous than just two warlocks working together. Dan was the face, Stewey the bones. Diviner and Enchanter.

All the Beijing folks back in Seattle expected a Chinese boy like him to be the expert on their history, when Dan preferred late Roman Empire and Dark Ages stuff. Stewey could read all the old stuff better than just about anybody Dan knew.

Today, they had a third with them. A Sorcerer more powerful than the two of them put together. Throw in a Conjurer, like he suspected Koschei was, and an Illusionist, and you just about had your bases covered. Assuming all the stories about Necromancers were more fable than truth.

What had Faucher been? The meditation maze in the back yard was pure enchantment, with some conjuring thrown in, opening portals to other places by walking through a shadow plane. The camouflage on the wall was a nice illusion but had leaked a little wrong.

Dan wondered if him breaking the meditation maze had overloaded the illusions in here and caused them to shift a little. Worth asking Stewey later.

And this wall was pure conjuration. Say the magic word, as it were, and open a portal, except he didn't know where it went.

Lots of power bound up right here, though.

"Stewey," Dan said as he walked around the fake wall on the floor and got a better look at the runes. "Can you read the path enchanted here?"

He felt both approach, different echoes in the way the magic around them flowed.

Stewey was as grounded as the earth. Maybe that was why his enchantments worked so well, if all magic that was lost went back underground?

Khulan reminded him of a bird, gliding on thermals, even inside this room.

Dan glanced back and returned her smile.

"Is Koschei Russian, like you?" he asked her.

"What?"

"You had to physically come here from somewhere else, when I broke the stepping disk," Dan explained. "That took time. Stewey just woke four people up downstairs, and I'm assuming you and Koschei are two of them. How long until someone could respond and find this wall?"

"The others might think it was a trap," she replied after a moment of thought. "They would divine, but it would take time for them to decide to approach. Days, not years. Probably not hours, unless one of them killed Faucher themselves and already knows what the barrier breaching implied. A spirit such as the one that attacked you earlier might come first, but those are from the darkness, and the sun is arisen."

"Then we have eight to ten hours before we could expect an ambush?" he asked her.

Her face got cuter when she got confused. More innocent and human, and less like an angry god forced to walk among peons like him and Stewey.

"Most likely, yes," she answered finally.

Dan smiled.

"Stewey, how hard will it be to open this thing and peek inside?" he asked.

"You are completely, fucking insane, Dr. Holt," Stewey said.

He always got serious when the situation did.

"Agreed, Dr. Ogden," Dan replied evenly. "But we have a day before someone shows up to steal anything. And a month before we have to repair this wall or the Grimsbys will own the place. They'll never see the portal like we do, but I could see them gutting this room and turning it into an arboretum or back into a patio. They've got the money."

"Step through an unknown portal, onto fuck only knows what kind of demiplane, engage whoever has been conjured to protect it, and escape safely afterwards?" Stewey asked in a blunt, disbelieving voice.

"You think that shadow servant will politely take no for an answer and not bother us again?" Dan asked.

Stewey surprised him by turning to Khulan.

"How powerful are you really, lady?" he asked her bluntly.

Stewey usually got tongue-tied around pretty women, so Dan was impressed. His anger must have overcome his embarrassment.

Khulan studied Dan's partner for a long second before she spoke.

"Near the top, Stewey," she said simply. "Those four names are probably interchangeable, but everyone else, everyone you would know, is down at least one entire step from that. The tradeoff is that I'm not prepared to do something like this today. Otherwise, I'd be wearing an enchanted scale armor and carrying a sword comparable to the old legends of Excalibur."

Dan started to say something tart and sarcastic, then realized that she might have been around at the time. Might have actually known Merlin and Morgan, or whatever they had been when those legends weren't legends.

And how much magic had been bound up in such a sword?

"We've got one chance," Dan said. "After that, I expect competition. We can't even run back to Seattle for anything good, lest someone figure it all out."

"Oh, I'm not completely at sea, Dr. Holt." Stewey suddenly grinned. "We did bring Bessie, after all. Be right back."

And he was out the door at a jog, footsteps receding.

Dan found himself alone with a being who claimed to be a goddess. Certainly the baddest warlock he'd ever met. The flower she had shown him in his mind was evidence of that. At the same time, he didn't think she had compromised him when she touched him.

Or if she did, she really was a god of some sort, and he and Stewey were just doomed.

"What will he return with?" she asked, maybe a little nervous now.

Stewey could do that to a person when he was on a role.

"Probably a heavy pistol loaded with silver bullets and a shotgun designed to deal with eldritch creatures and conjurations," Dan said, reaching for the knife he had stowed and holding it out to her. "You a better knife fighter than I am?"

"Keep it," she said. "It's bound to you already, so I'd be fighting it as much as anything I tried to stab."

"Bound to me?" Dan asked.

He watched her hold out a hand and cast a small divination, letting it float towards him like a spider web. Dan saw it land and the knife glowed, about like he expected.

Except that his hand and arm did as well.

All the way up to his shoulder, which was about where he'd gone numb when he stabbed that shadow servant.

"How'd that happen?" he asked blankly.

"Kill anything powerful recently with the blade?" she asked in a scientific tone utterly at odds with a conversation on magic and eldritch creatures.

"Your stepping disk," Dan said automatically. "And I stabbed that damned creature last night. This morning. Whenever."

"Well, you stole some of his energy when you did," she nodded. "And perhaps some of the disk's, as well."

"Huh," Dan grunted. "And you're walking in there with us?"

"As you said, this might be the only chance to do this before someone else gets in and discovers whatever secrets Faucher left behind."

"Is this the dumbest idea you've ever heard?" Dan had to ask.

"Not even in the top ten, Dan," she smiled back at him. "There's probably a guardian of some sort, but there are three of us. My greater fear is that Koschei was already coming here, the same as I was, and is waiting for us when we emerge."

"Anything we can do to mess with his plans?" Dan turned back and studied the wall.

Up close, the bricks were just exactly like they had been when the building was raised. He could taste the age of the bricks themselves, and they had been reclaimed from an older building, a factory of some sort down closer to Seattle.

Dan placed his free hand on the wall, unwilling to put the knife down, and cast a Knowing into the wall.

Taylor, Washington. He had the coordinates in his head of a town that had been erased, and all the buildings torn down. The bricks of one of the factories there had ended up here somehow. Nothing magical about them except the immense age of good, red brick that would outlast them all.

He turned and glanced at Khulan.

Most of them.

The portal existed as a layer of frosting over the wall, if you could call it that. Again, the Grimsbys would see nothing, even if the wall wasn't repaired later. You had to have opened yourself to the power to sense it, and it was luck and the combination of a Diviner, an Enchanter, and a Sorcerer to open this up correctly.

Someone, Dan presumed Faucher had marked the wall in the shape of a classical Roman archway, about nine feet tall at the capstone and just over three feet wide. The underlying bricks anchored the magic itself, but Dan closed his eyes and pushed with his mind.

The wall didn't open, but he could see into the shadows beyond. A corridor, receding out of sight, but he could sense the first twist. It wasn't a square corner, like the role-playing maps he'd had as a kid, drawn on graph paper. Felt more like a French curve, sliding around an arc and then suddenly doubling back.

Dan blinked and stepped back.

"What is it?" Khulan asked, suddenly right at his elbow so close he had to turn his head without moving so he didn't run right into one of her breasts.

"Looked inside the portal." Dan breathed heavily. "Got a taste of the interior, even though I couldn't see anything."

"And?" she asked, still way too close to a relative stranger.

"Labyrinth."

FIFTEEN

Khulan shuddered at the implications of the word. The British had absorbed and transmitted a wide variety of literary histories from their distant past, from the Romans to the ancient Egyptians. Along the way, they had rediscovered the Greeks, who had called themselves Hellenes.

Khulan and her forebears had been forest tribes far to the northeast, thousands and thousands of kilometers away from the fabled lands of Homer, but she had studied enough of the culture, itself transmitted along to the Sarmatians and through them to the Scythians and others.

A beast half-man and half-bull, imprisoned by order of the king of Crete in a maze so complicated that the creature known as the Minotaur could not escape. Young men and women sacrificed to the creature on a regular basis until one of the great heroes of Greek myth, Theseus, was able to destroy it.

She considered the wall the held the portal. Faucher had been a powerful Conjurer, even though she didn't know if that was his specialization. Certainly, the ability to ground a portal to a demiplane such as this was an expression of might. Especially as it had outlived him.

Had he protected the interior with a maze and a monster as well?

"What do we know?" Stewey's return interrupted her thoughts.

"Got a maze inside the portal, Stewey," Dan spoke up as she turned and stepped enough back that Dan wouldn't brush against her if he turned. "Labyrinth."

"Good thing I came prepared for minotaurs, then," he smiled as he approached.

Dan had been correct in his assumptions. Stewey had a large pistol holstered on his right thigh and a pump shotgun in both hands. A backpack presumably held all manner of gear, as Ogden had impressed her as the one who had a kit handy for emergencies at all times.

A bug-out bag, as some people called them.

He placed the shotgun carefully against the wall nearby and shrugged his way out of the pack. Unzipped, he began to rifle around inside until he pulled out a large spool of heavy,black thread, almost a spindle, and a nail, which he drove with a hammer into the remaining part of the wooden wall, next to the exposed brick.

Stewey tied one end of the thread to the nail and handed her the spool.

"Dan will be on point watching," he explained. "I'll be ready to shoot anything that moves. You unwind this as we go, taking care not to break it. There's five hundred yards, and I've got two more in case, plus some rope."

Khulan wasn't sure she wanted to know why, but

supposed that he had a sewing kit in there. Still, it made sense.

Theseus had supposedly been able to find his way back out of the labyrinth because he had a similar device.

"And you think that a shotgun will protect you against magical creatures?" Khulan tried not to sneer, but it still came out harsh and abrasive.

That was mostly the goddess talking.

Ogden surprised her by grinning like the fabled Cheshire cat of English legend.

"Three-inch magnum loads," he said, like she would be able to penetrate his nerdiness. "Number two shot with a little of everything mixed in."

"Everything?" she asked perhaps still a little ruder than the situation warranted.

"Silver drop shot," he explained. "Cold iron. Marble. Glass. Wood. Mistletoe. Hell, I've even got tiny beads of Jell-O made with holy water. If it has magical allergies, I've tried to cover it. And the even-numbered rounds on the pistol will go through a Class II armored limousine at close enough range."

"Why?" she asked, finally more confused than insulted.

"Stewey expects Bigfoot to come for his stamp collection," Dan explained.

Must be an inside joke, because it went right over Khulan's head, even as Stewey practically preened.

Still, the two humans believed that they were prepared for what they would find on Faucher's demiplane. They probably weren't, but would be counting on her to assist.

Khulan wanted to know the man's secrets, too. Especially if he had chosen the same path as the goddess, having finally worn out the flesh.

She studied the spindle of thread in her hands. Heavy cotton. Rugged stuff you might make a jacket out of, rather than something light and pretty. It conveyed a brutal, no-nonsense approach that reminded her of the man who had handed it to her.

Dan was the one with the light, delicate touch. The Air, if you wanted to also go back to those silly Hellenes and their elementalism approach.

Stewey was most definitely Earth in that reference.

That would make her Water, flowing around barriers such as death, rather than beating her heads relentlessly against it down the centuries.

Water, bringer of life in the form of the rains that fell and gave life to the great Yenisei River, flowing north into the icelands. Cold and quiet and deadly.

Yes, she felt the cold waters and snows of her homeland.

Did that make Faucher Fire?

Or Koschei?

"I'm ready," she said simply, nodding to the two men once she had gotten her head wrapped around the stupidity of this undertaking. "Should I open the portal, or will one of you?"

"I'll do it," Dan said. "My assumption is that your friend left more traps behind, like the four names on the front door. We need to slide by them, rather than just bashing them down. At least most of the time."

Khulan agreed. It was a sound strategy, if Kai Faucher

had indeed left this all as a trap for her or one of the others.

But she was still more powerful.

And had brought along a capable pair of friends.

She took a breath and pulled as much magic out of the walls and mansion as she could and watched Dan open the portal into darkness.

SIXTEEN

Dan concentrated on the portal. This wasn't like the meditation maze, where the power pulled your down under the water like a siren drowning sailors. Faucher had left that thing in place and let it do most of the work, so that someone entering would have already forced it open by the time they arrived at the center.

Here, the door was hidden behind an illusion that probably had been slightly misaligned by the flow of magic the broken stepping disk had released, or he might never had found it. With the wall gone, the Grimsbys wouldn't have noticed anything awry, but he'd been able to identify it.

The portal itself felt heavy, like a solid slab of granite. But the magic was also almost perfectly balanced, like that granite had been resting on the exquisite pins and could be pushed in without a lot of work.

Dan wasn't sure if that was so Faucher could get in quickly, or it was a trap designed to lure sailors to their doom. At least they would have the thread if the door closed behind them, and the maze started playing tricks.

Hopefully, they wouldn't find a minotaur inside who snuck up and cut it with his axe.

Anything was possible when you went and carved out your own demiplane from the essence of raw chaos. You could fill it with whatever spirits you could summon and convince to populate the place.

Dan had heard lurid tales of some of the more *interesting* ideas that powerful Conjurers had come up with over the centuries. The sorts of things you got when emotionally-stunted nerds with power went off the rails.

He peered into the darkness beyond a hole in the universe and sniffed.

Old, wet stone. The kind that had a seep because it was underground and not quite sealed against water. Or humidity was too great, and you got indoor dew.

There was a musky smell underneath it all that Dan couldn't identify, except that it probably marked the guardian.

He turned to Khulan and studied her closely. She was wound as tight as a Swiss watch, but probably was about as reliable, too, from the calmness she exuded.

He could work with that.

"How grown-up was Faucher?" he asked. "We dealing with an old scholar or a punk spellblaster?"

"Meaning?" she looked up at him with eyes he swore glowed blue for a moment before returning to jade.

"I'm thinking Minotaur," Dan said. "Labyrinth and all that. Old scholar. If he was still a punk kid with power, should we be prepared for a succubus or a chain maiden?"

From the way her teeth clenched and her jaw muscles stood out, Dan presumed that Faucher wasn't the scholarly type. The sour note on her face spoke volumes.

"Anything that moves, Dan," she said simply. "Nothing in there is going to be friendly, until one of us banishes it and summons our own version. Our own binding."

"Gotcha," he said. "Stewey, you heard the lady."

"Did," the man said. "You remember to duck if something steps out. Not feeling all that chivalristic today."

Dan nodded.

*Kill them all and MAKE God sort them out, since that was **Her** job*, as Stewey liked to frame it when he was feeling exceptionally rude.

Just because, Dan led with the knife, feeling it pierce the boundary between worlds with the slightest pop. He followed it in and entered a stereotypical cut-stone room right out of a movie.

Rather than bricks, the interior was comprised of dressed stones in dark gray about a foot on a side and mortared in place. When he glanced back, he saw he was a few inches from the room outside and the air in here was warmer. Almost enough to take off his shell, but he figured he'd rather sweat right now.

The knife glowed, ever so slightly, but the room itself had a soft ambiance. As he took a second step, more of the room came into focus, and he saw oil lamps hanging from wrought iron sconces on the side walls.

So, an illusion on top of everything else?

Dan paused and summoned as much magic as he could to him. It was much easier here, telling him that this place was outside the plane he knew and closer to…someplace.

The magic had a taste like you got when you touched your tongue to a nine volt battery, electricy and sharp.

Not quite tainted, but closer to the font of whatever chaos it drew from. Or maybe magic on earth had been filtered by the land itself and neutralized?

He cast a Knowing and pushed it all directions like a sonar ping, listening for whatever echoes returned.

The demiplane was less than a mile on a side, maybe all on one level more or less, but he couldn't tell more than that. Merely how far out that the barriers of chaos had grown strong enough to consume his signal. Nothing was close, and the room had a single door on the far wall, oak boards banded with cold iron and etched with silver runes.

Designed to keep something on the other side.

Dan turned back and Khulan had a waviness to her appearance, as though he was underwater in a pool looking up at her. He gestured for her to join him, unsure if sound would cross the barrier any clearer than light would.

She had the spool of thread in one hand and unrolled it as she walked.

The barrier fought her for just a second, but then failed and she was suddenly clear, standing next to him.

"You okay?" Dan asked.

"Yes," she replied, shaking her head to test it. "We will need to map this space later, to see if we can enter from another direction."

"You can do that?" Dan heard his voice go up.

"Dream thieves," she replied obscurely. "That's how they work."

Whatever that meant. Sounded like something he'd need to learn about, if he and Stewey were going to survive in the big leagues.

Seattle hadn't felt like bush leagues before now, but maybe it was.

Stewey was checking the thread from the outside, but he seemed convinced, so he entered a moment later, bulling his way through the barrier like a man in a Tuff Mudder run on the home stretch.

"Nifty," he said with a bright grin, turning all directions to look, including back above the doorway, just in case something was lurking there.

Anybody else and Dan would be concerned, but Stewey was the safest person he knew with a gun.

Never point it at something until you're ready to kill them with it.

Stewey smiled like he was reading Dan's mind, and racked the first of five rounds into the weapon, pausing to slide a round into the magazine tube underneath.

"First load is shot," he announced in an offhand voice. "Second penetrates armor."

"What kind of armor?" Khulan turned to ask.

"An armored car door," Stewey said. "The asshole behind the door wearing a Class III vest. The asshole next to him, also wearing a vest. The armored door on the far side of the vehicle. That help?"

Magnum slugs. Handloaded by a man convinced he might need to shoot down a helicopter at some point. Or a dragon.

Or, as Stewey would say: *Ain't no extra credit for neatness.*

The portal was not a physical barrier, so Dan was able to push it closed with his magic, leaving it just enough open that it didn't cut the thread connecting them to the real world.

He positioned the other two where he wanted them and approached the second, inner door.

Khulan was dead center of the room, practically glowing with the amount of power she was holding. She rested the spool in her back pocket and cast a blur that put his to shame. In her left hand, a blade of pure blackness appeared, like a hungry shadow, nearly a yard long.

Stewey was on the shield side of her, back and over a step where he could shoot without hitting her and would be lined up with the door gap as Dan opened it, knife in hand.

That thing was a bank vault cast in wood. Five feet wide. Eleven feet tall. Felt like a foot thick, with bands across at three levels, wrought in iron and with silver runes that pulsed as he got close.

"Whatever is on the other side is not getting past this," Dan said, studying the power contained here. "If we open it, we might let something out. If we close it behind us, are we trapped here?"

Khulan cast something that hung on the inside of the door like a neon green spider web.

"It contains a single name," she said. "So presumably the Minotaur cannot escape. Perhaps we could also bind the creature with it later, depending."

Dan didn't see any locks on the door, just a brass

handle to turn and pull. He grasped the cool metal and turned it just enough to confirm that he could. The room in here was just bright enough to read by, but not much more.

"Opening the door now," he said in a clear voice.

He pulled, but the door didn't want to move. There was enough magic floating around in here that he grabbed a hunk and focused it into the interior of the door itself to look.

Just heavy and a tight fit.

Dan jerked it hard and felt it scrape against the frame as it opened.

The smell inside was cooler and drier. Muskier, too, like whoever it was occasionally walked up to the other side of the door but wasn't able to get through. That was good.

And bad. That meant that he probably was going to run into something at some point.

If not *someone*.

The corridor receded into the distance, broken by more oil lamps, but these had a magical taste that told him they were illusions.

Good enough to light the way but not needing someone to service them.

Nothing jumped out at them.

Dan remembered to breathe.

He studied the other side of the door. Cold iron handle, the kind worked by a patient blacksmith Enchanter rather than being poured out of a forge. What Stewey could create if he got motivated. Or pissed.

Proof against a broad variety of fay and eldritch creatures, so Dan assumed that the guardian had been conjured, rather than trained. A spirit given flesh and purpose by someone like Faucher for purposes Dan hoped weren't prurient.

He really didn't want to deal with a demon babe today, in any of the forms a horny old goat might decide to shape.

"Stepping through," Dan said. "You stay here, and I'll see if I can open it."

That would leave him alone against whatever denizens were here, but keep the other two safe.

"I'm coming with you," Khulan announced. "Stewey can protect the rear."

Dan caught Stewey's blush but didn't say anything. His partner was back to being flustered by pretty women, which was better than letting his overall grumpiness at the situation rule things.

Dan nodded and stepped into the corridor beyond. The ceiling felt like fog but was still there if he pushed his senses upward. Just obscured by a malignant mist hanging in the air.

Khulan joined him a second later and the whole sense of dread he had felt seemed to drift away from him, like a fan pushing smoke. She must be doing something. Or maybe was just that powerful.

The stone underfoot was rough, polished enough to be smooth but not reflective. Good grip for his shoes, if he needed to maneuver quickly. The walls were the same one-foot blocks inset with mortar.

Dan reached back and grasped the handle, pulling the door closed. Felt like a bank vault closing as it did.

He turned to where Khulan was watching the middle distance. Almost sniffing the air.

Maybe daring whatever was there to come over here and get its ass kicked.

At least she had that black sword and her blur ready for combat.

Dan had played enough *Dungeons and Dragons* as a kid to understand his role here. He was the thief. Khulan was the fighter. Stewey was a ranger or maybe a cleric, considering all the stuff he had to buff with in those pockets.

Oh, but for a light crossbow right now. And some studded leather armor.

Hell, why not wish for a tank to drive down these corridors, spewing silver cannon rounds at whatever moved?

"All good?" he asked, checking that the brick-babe with the nice bottom would protect his back when he turned it.

"I am prepared," she said in some weirdly formal way.

Back to the goddess talking, and not the hot blonde chick.

Too bad.

Dan grasped the handle lightly, just in case it would zap him, but nothing happened. He turned it and pushed, jacking his weight into it, expecting that moment of friction against the doorway.

It slid open and Stewey had the shotgun not quite pointed at his face.

"Dr. Livingston, I presume?" he asked.

"Very funny, Stewey," Dan answered, looking down to see that the thread was still intact.

"Man's got to be prepared," Stewey grinned, following Dan back into the outer corridor and pulling the door shut to keep whoever trapped in the labyrinth.

Dan took a deep breath and moved to the front of the line again.

The corridor wasn't straight, but that was not clear, looking at it. But they weren't necessarily in a Cartesian world now, so physics could be bent. The corridor scrolled slowly to the right, much like the opening of the medication maze outside had.

But Dan had already seen the first fork in his mind. Given enough time, he might be able to conjure a tiny eyeball and send it roaming down every pathway until it found the center.

Or the Minotaur.

That still sounded better than walking into the beast.

"I'm going to try something," Dan said before he took a step deeper into the mudpit of his day.

"Got you covered," Stewey called.

Khulan remained so silent that he had to turn to see her nod.

Outside the world. Close by to lots and *lots* of chaos.

Playing in the big leagues now. And maybe a computer game he remembered.

He sat and crossed his legs, just because this would take a lot of concentration and he didn't want to fall over when he did it.

Dan closed his eyes and thought of the sorts of spells you cast when you wanted to bring a shadow to life.

Those were hard unless you had the gift. At most, you got a little mouse of a creature that couldn't lift more than a pencil.

Not like that stupid beast that had broken into the office last night.

He didn't need a monster here. Just something he could send ahead.

For grins, he concentrated on a variant of a Japanese demon he'd seen in a manga once. Reached out and grabbed a great big handful of the chaos swirling around outside this maze and squished it together into a lump about as big as a golf ball, chanting quietly under his breath.

Still took a lot of effort. Drained juice out of him as well as what he'd gathered.

Dan opened his hands and tossed it into the air, the universe's ugliest Tinkerbelle.

It was an eyeball, with a tiny stub of a torso coming out the bottom where two spindly arms hung.

Jade green iris. He hoped she didn't catch an association.

It turned and smiled at him with a mouth that took up the bottom part of the ball.

Blinked once with its whole body in the weirdest way.

"Go," Dan commanded it lightly. "Seek and return."

Zip. Gone like the *Road Runner* cartoon. He kept expecting a tongue to come out.

Dan took a deep breath and flexed stiff shoulders. He put a hand down to pick up his knife and stood up like an old man.

"Now what?" Stewey asked.

"Now we wait," Khulan-the-maybe-goddess replied. "The watcher will find the monster or be destroyed by it."

Dan shrugged. Not like it was a real creature. Just a puff of chaos magic he'd twisted into shape for a task, so if it went bang, he wasn't out anything.

He pushed his mind outward, and it was suddenly like he was riding shotgun, back when Stewey still that '72 Chevelle SS with the overbuilt engine and a blower that sounded like an angry dragon as he hit one hundred and forty on a straightaway outside Yakima.

You could see what was in front of you, but the sides were just a blur.

Dan felt a hand on his arm.

"Are you well?" Khulan whispered into his ear.

"Riding the watcher," he said, hoping it made sense.

"There is a technique," she said. "Close one eye."

Didn't make any sense, but Dan did as she bade him.

Suddenly, he was in both places. Still blasting too fast down stone hallways but looking at her from close enough that he'd have fogged her glasses if she wore any.

"Wow," he managed.

"I forget that you are still young in the arts," the goddess said. "There is much I could teach you, when it is safer."

That sounded exhilarating and dangerous, all at once.

Road Runner wasn't trying to think his way through the maze, just go down every corridor until it dead-ended and then backtrack. It had enough bloodhound in him to always find the spot. And it felt like they were moving at Chevelle speeds right now, daring the coyote to chase him around corners and off cliffs.

Dan was still a little woozy, but standing helped, and he could feel the energy of the maze flowing back into him, leaving him maybe a little punch-drunk with power.

He had a knife. And a babe. And a Stewey.

Bring it.

The little eyeball finally found the center of the maze. Slammed square into an invisible barrier so hard he went flat like a racquetball and bounced off, spinning like he was in a cartoon.

"Whoo." Dan felt the room turn under his feet until he closed both his eyes.

They approached the second time at little-old-lady-driving speeds, one spindly arm with two fingers and a thumb out in front until the found the window.

Tapped it lightly.

Magic so intense that it was like stone.

Somebody didn't want to be bothered by peons and eyeballs.

Then it stirred, whatever *it* was.

Hissed in the distance, although Dan wasn't sure how he and his buddy heard it.

Didn't matter.

Road Runner was off like he was trying to make the jump to light speed, and Dan was along for the ride.

He opened both his eyes to see Khulan watching him and Stewey prepared to unleash redneck mayhem.

"Wow," Dan managed as he got his thoughts organized. "Don't need the thread. We could actually navigate the whole place."

"We?" Khulan was a step back, and her blur was between them.

"Me and the eyeball," Dan hastened to add. "He moves like a Road Runner, but also navigated this whole side of the maze just like that. Found something, too."

Dan felt a ping, like a kitty meowing quietly.

"Stewey, my eyeball wants to come in from the cold," Dan said. "Please don't shoot him when he does."

"You know it's still yours?" Stewey asked in an authoritative voice.

"Meep meep," Dan laughed.

He looked down the corridor and saw an eyeball peeked around a corner at them, like in a cartoon.

"It's safe," Dan called.

The eyeball moved from cover and approached at what he probably thought was a slow walk. Stewey was tracking it all the way with the shotgun.

It stopped and looked up at Dan in confusion.

He'd known dogs that would cock their head at an angle when they didn't understand. It was weird watching an eyeball do it.

Then the little creature spun in place to look backwards, made a chirping sound, and scampered behind Dan, climbing up on his shoulder like a parrot and holding on to an ear.

Stewey relented from pointed the shotgun in Dan's face and pivoted back to the corridor as a sound emerged from the depths.

Khulan moved to one side and took up a guard position where Dan and Stewey could both act but be protected.

And the road runner.

Dan noticed a glow approaching.

CHAPTER

SEVENTEEN

Khulan had not expected Faucher to have built something this complex and devious, but her dealings with the man had been mostly through intermediaries and neutral third parties, not face-to-face.

This demiplane showed a level of power and sophistication that suggested the stepping disk was a negligible thing, rather than the acme of his art.

She smelled something coming towards them down the hallway. Dan's watcher spirit had almost no smell, so she knew it wasn't that. And the door containing only one name suggested strongly that Faucher had bound a single guardian for this place.

The real question was whether Faucher was still alive and had faked his own death to hide here for a time. Or perhaps left this for his successor and passed his memories and power onto a newer body.

You couldn't truly command a new soul if you tried to ride it, but you could pick something with a weak mind and browbeat it into submission.

The goddess had always chosen from among the strongest of her willing acolytes, both of mind and spirit, as well as power. Khulan was honored to be her mount for her lifetime.

A sound reached out as the creature approached.

Khulan couldn't make out the words, but the ethereal beauty of the song itself was something she had never encountered in her five millennia on this earth. She paused and listened.

Another goddess emerged from the distant gloom, tall and gorgeous and cloaked in white silk robes that flowed around her like creatures. Khulan felt short and ugly by comparison to the woman, but she knew that the goddess approaching loved her.

Would always love her. Would bring her joy and glory through her entire life.

The weapons were not needed, so Khulan released the blade of darkness back to its home and unspun the blur. Without that, the goddess could approach them, and they could all bask in her glory and love.

Golden eyes met hers and swelled until Khulan felt like she would fall into them forever. She felt the hurt in the woman that the two men did not trust her. Nor in the goddess.

They would hurt the women, because they were children with too much power.

Khulan understood that she should protect the goddess from these men, and then she wouldn't have to share the goddess's love with mere mortals who had no understanding of true love.

A sound filled Khulan's head with pain. The world

itself shattered into a thousand fragments of glass that fell to the stone floor and ruptured further.

The goddess screamed, driving Khulan to her knees with both hands ineffectually trying to cover her ears.

Another sound Khulan could not recognize.

Another scream.

The goddess demanded that Khulan protect her, as the men had turned and were going to destroy all the beauty in the world, as the moderns did.

Magic would be gone, and even the ancients would no longer be able to sustain themselves.

A dragon roared nearby and the goddess before her suddenly turned to darkness and rage, screaming as it ran from them, the silken robes turning to rusty chains.

Khulan blinked as everything receded.

"And stay gone, bitch," an angry voice growled.

Khulan saw something on the floor as she knelt. She picked it up with unknowing hands and turned it over, but cognition would not come.

"You two okay?" the voice demanded, cutting through the glaze of honey that had coated her mind.

Khulan looked up at Stewey, and everything washed off her like rain.

"What happened?" she asked as she rose, handing Stewey the fired shotgun shell, still smoking.

"Chain maiden," the redneck growled in a tone so angry that she thought she could see sparks coming off his skin. "Promise you all sorts of things so they can get close. They'll love you forever, if you just serve them. Crap like that."

Khulan shook her head to clear the cobwebs and

summoned her blur again, twisting it this time to protect her from sound as well. She'd never encountered a chain maiden before, apparently. They weren't prevalent in the places where she had been, so she assumed them to be a Western thing. Perhaps an American thing.

The sword returned to her a moment later, hungry for souls to steal.

"How were you able to resist it?" she asked Stewey.

He got an angry, terrible scowl on his face unlike anything she had ever imagined the man might contain. So bad, she took a half step back and wondered if he was about to shoot her, but the moment passed.

"They don't really care that you're rich," he snarled. "Never. The money means nothing to them. At least until you get closer and find that they're just gold-diggers sniffing for a payday."

At least his face cleared, and he turned to stare at the corridor where the creature had fled.

"Bitch, you better find a way to escape, before I catch you," he muttered just loud enough that Khulan could understand the words.

She turned to Dan, standing on her other side and also recovering from the song of a land Siren. A Chain maiden.

Dan and the eyeball spirit were shaken. Amazingly, the eyeball had not been disrupted when Dan was subject to the woman's song.

Khulan would have expected the creature to vanish in a puff of smoke. Dan must have done a better job that either of them had been expecting.

"Are you okay?" Dan asked carefully.

"That was the most beautiful thing I have ever heard,"

Khulan admitted. "Won't work a second time, as I've added her song to the blur. You should to the same."

"Song?" his face showed surprise. "You can blur sound as well?"

It struck her then just how far out of their depth these two men really were. Or perhaps not, considering that Stewey had saved them and not her.

Unknowledgeable, which was not the same thing as ignorant.

They both contained enormous potential, but nobody they knew had the power to train them properly.

Dare she?

She had known them for less than a day, but both had proven worthy companions in that time, and she had taken measures to *Know* them magically as well as socially.

Khulan took her blur and held it out to Dan, like it was a physical shield, rather than a magical creation.

"Take this," she ordered. "You'll be able to hold it long enough before it fails. That will show you how."

Dan did. From the look on his face, it was probably like trying to hold a cat that didn't want to be touched, but he managed to bring it to rest on his fist and actually grip the thing for several seconds.

"Oh!" his eyes lit up and he let go his concentration. "Like this."

And his own blur appeared in its place. This one was larger than she had expected him to control. And it had a blue tone that was rare. Most of them were the gray of light and dark mixed. Being and Chaos blending slowly.

Blur.

Stewey gave her a good dose of side-eye, but he probably didn't trust any woman right now, based on the history he had just revealed.

That was fine. She didn't find him all that interesting and was already so wealthy he wouldn't believe it if she told him.

"Bitch can't escape the labyrinth," Stewey announced, reloading his shotgun and collecting the two spent rounds from the floor. "Do we chase her or just drive her off from the central plaza?"

"Sam ran into a barrier around the plaza," Dan replied. "If we can get her away from it and get to the heart, she can have this place. Worse come to worst, we can break the portal magic and seal the place up."

"No," Khulan corrected him. "If she really angers me, I can unmake this place. Not today, but once I'm home and have all my tools handy. Who is Sam?"

The eyeball popped out from behind Dan's ear and blinked his whole body at her.

Dan pointed at the creature.

"Sam," he introduced them.

The creature had enough awareness of the world to bow to her and wave at Stewey. Probably the correct response to both, although she had never encountered such a raised creature with that acuity.

Dan probably didn't realize what he'd done. That might become important later, but for now she nodded to the watcher and turned to look into the distance.

"Let us see if she wishes to try her luck a second time," Khulan said, gesturing for Dan and Sam to precede her.

EIGHTEEN

Dan could smell the musk that the chain maiden had left behind.

The creature couldn't bleed. Not really, but Stewey had ruptured its hide with shot, so there was something in those loads she wouldn't like. Something that would hurt her.

And he had learned a nifty new magical trick from Khulan. His blur was more powerful than it had been before because he'd been doing it wrong.

Well, not wrong, but there was an extra icon you could add to the runes in your mind when you cast it that made it larger and tougher.

And it protected you from singing vampires.

That would be useful later. They sang and you were suddenly in love with them. Wanted to do anything you could for them.

Right up to the point that they got close enough to wrap you in those chains, kill you, and eat you.

He should be dead. Bush league stupid. But Khulan

had also gotten knocked on her ass by the demon, so maybe they were all bush league.

But for Stewey, he'd be someone's lunch right now. Of course, how many times had that been the truth?

One crazed redneck Enchanter, who was probably worth his weight in gold and not just for being prepared to kill a chain maiden.

"Sam," Dan said, turning his head and feeling the hand detach.

His friendly eyeball floated over in front of him, looking like nothing so much as a puppy that knew piddling on the carpet was bad, but hadn't been able to help himself.

"No, I don't want you too far out front, either," Dan reassured the little pixie demonling. "Just off to one side and out of Stewey's way so he doesn't shoot you. Okay?"

The little eyeball nodded and blinked. Dan would have said hitched up his pants, but the thing didn't even have legs, let alone clothes.

Still, Dan caught a huff of toughness as Sam drifted over to the left wall and stayed low to the ground, like a rabbit on guard duty.

Dan walked on the right side, where the blur would be in the middle, and he had both Khulan and Stewey close enough if she decided to come back for more.

The chain maiden had been hurt. Dan had felt the impact of buckshot ripping demonic skin and letting ichor drop out, even if none of it stayed material long enough to stain the floor.

"Let's go," he said to the other two.

Other three. He had a familiar or something right

now, so he'd count Sam until the summoning eventually faded.

Sam had zoomed half the labyrinth at crazy high speed, but Dan could easily remember which branches to take, in order to get to the central plaza where the guardian had been resting before.

Nobody knew if she'd want to come back for a second round, when the invaders had shown that they could threaten her very existence.

Just how suicidal did your summoning bind you, lady?

Dan sniffed the air. Brimstone, for lack of a better term, instead of the nice musk of a beautiful woman that had been there before, so either she was more badly hurt than Dan had thought, or had given up all pretense of sexy and was just going to jump out and try to strangle someone with those chains.

"What's the reach of a chain maiden?" Dan asked in general, pursuing a thread.

"Do I look like an expert Conjurer, Dr. Holt?" Stewey growled back.

"De-Conjurer." Dan laughed. "Banisher, maybe. Khulan?"

"I have never encountered such a creature," she replied. "What are you thinking?"

"Baiting her," Dan said, sounding far more confident than he felt. "Leading you by a bit more than might be safe, to see if she'll try her luck on me, where you two can still nail her ass to a wall if she does."

"Does Sam bite?" Stewey laughed back.

Dan joined the laughter at the look of utter horror

than a face made up of nothing but an eyeball could convey.

Window to the soul, indeed.

Maybe next time he'd look to summon the soul of a wolverine, instead of a wombat.

"Not too far," Dan said. "You two stay close together as well, and Sam and I will scout a little."

Dan moved forward until he was about twenty yards ahead, and then gestured for Khulan and Stewey to follow. He wasn't moving all that fast. Sam was almost sleepwalking across from him, but he knew where he was going.

First branch choice. There were no pit traps that Sam had been able to detect, but the eyeball had also been flying, so he wouldn't have found a false stone.

The right led to a long dead-end with nothing interesting. Dan chose the left, watching the floor and relying on Sam to watch for tripwires or something at ankle level.

He heard a sound in the long distance. Not a woman singing, but perhaps crying. Like she'd been hurt and needed you to comfort her.

Almost as good a trap, except that his blur was deflecting it. Which meant…

Dan turned back and gestured to Khulan, tapping his ear, but she was already casting a spell of some sort over Stewey, leaving him with a green glow that Dan could see from here.

"He's deaf for now," she called quietly. "Man won't put the shotgun down to cast his own blur, so he cannot hear anything, but he's aware of that."

Stewey nodded, as if he could sense what they were saying.

Dan held up a thumb rather than answering. Deaf Stewey against chain maiden song wasn't even remotely a fair fight, but he'd be happy sending her back to hell to commiserate with her fellow demons for a while.

Down the left corridor when it forked. The singing got a little louder but remained distant. Dan wondered if that was the improved blur, keeping her magic at a distance, rather than letting it infect his mind.

Nobody likes hearing a woman cry. Man's almost programmed to want to do something about it.

In this case, shove a knife into her throat and saw, but maybe Dan didn't have the purest motives.

The corridors got twisty. Nothing like he'd drawn on graph paper as a kid. More organic. Designed to confuse someone who hadn't sent a road runner down them once already to memorize them and let him see the path.

One thing was certain, Dan knew he'd stepped up a notch in power, just in the last day. Where that was taking them was hard to guess, but if he wanted to play in the big leagues, you had to spend a season in Visalia first.

The singing faded after a time. Must have realized that it wasn't working.

Could demons learn to fear?

Might be a good time to see.

Dan paused.

"Trying something stupid," he said to Khulan, smiling as he already knew what Stewey would say.

You are completely fucking insane, Dr. Holt.

Not the most original line. Not even particularly wrong this time.

Dan was surrounded by chaos. Raw magical energy that contained everything else, if the ancient theories were correct, where humans and gods had carved out order and rules.

Chaos still bled in, which was why everything wasn't static and boring, but it got *filtered*.

There were precious few filters around him right now.

Cole had always said that the real limits on magic were how little of it was left in the world these days. Your imagination could do anything, if you could find a big enough powersink to draw from. That was why wizards enchanted wands, swords, and stones.

You could hold more power that way.

How much power had gotten trapped in old items, instead of recycled? Or in maintaining people who should be dead, like this Koschei dude. Or Faucher?

Was the secret to saving the world of magic wrapped up in breaking things, rather than hoarding them?

Crap, he'd never imagined that sort of future.

But right now, he was floating in a box at sea, surrounded by raw power so intense that his teeth had started to hurt.

He was a Diviner. A warlock sensitive to the ebb and flow of magic and its interaction with the world.

What were the limits to his imagination?

"Keep watch," he said to Sam, who nodded shakily, like he could read Dan's mind and was afraid to be collateral damage.

You're safe, Sam.

Dan drew a breath in hard. Pulled as much magic with it as he could hold. It felt like he'd just eaten the whole salad, a thirty-two-ounce prime rib, all the bread, and ordered dessert, too.

He closed his eyes and *pushed*.

The stones beneath his feet began to glow. Not golden bricks, but the effect was similar. A path six feet wide, running right now the middle of the corridor, except where it branched around traps that were suddenly obvious.

Dan twisted the magic and locked it to the ground. You could do that with enough chaos handy.

And the will.

He felt twenty pounds lighter when he breathed again, but the path was obvious now. And would be to anyone entering the labyrinth.

Chain maidens be damned.

Dan turned to Khulan and smiled. She had a look of newly-found respect in her eyes.

Stewey seemed to be laughing, but made no more sound than he heard.

Sam winked. Or blinked. Hard to tell with just one eye.

Dan started forward, walking carefully around the spot where a panel would fall out of the floor like an airlock opening to drop you into deep space.

Except that it would plunge you into raw chaos, which would probably be something more like acid.

Another place would drop a portcullis from the ceiling, presumably so you couldn't escape the bitch summoned as a guardian.

Like he wanted to.

He owed her almost as much as Stewey did.

They arrived at the place where Sam had bounced. To Dan, it was like a glass door had been closed, but he understood that Faucher was hiding the last secret within.

The singing had stopped, but Dan didn't know if she had fled to the furthest reaches of the labyrinth or was lurking just inside the door for him to get within reach.

He felt Stewey tap him on the shoulder.

When he turned. Stewey handed him the shotgun with a nod and pulled a rock hammer from one of his pockets. A rock hammer?

It was like that BBC SciFi character with the long coat and the famous scarf, forever pulling oddities from a pocket.

Dan stepped to one side and nodded for Sam to stand clear and keep watch. Khulan was lurking near to Stewey like a guardian reaper, that terrible black sword almost humming with excitement.

He hoped it was the sword, and not the woman holding it.

Dan knew how to use the shotgun. Stewey had made sure they spent regular time on a shooting range. Dan wasn't into skeet, but that wasn't the same as incapable. Stewey was just such a deadeye shot that any competition with the man was a waste of time.

Unless Dan could find a sucker.

Stewey walked to the edge of the doorway and studied it while his two protectors—three—watched over him.

Dan knew that he should be able to see through the

door, but the illusion in place was so thick that it was like fog made solid.

He watched Stewey tap the door frame silently with his little hammer. Softly. Like you'd play a xylophone.

He moved to the other side, ducking under Dan's barrel, and tapping again.

Nothing happened, but Stewey seemed pleased. He slid back out of the way and put a hand on Dan's arm. Dan handed him the shotgun, and then got ushered back. Khulan got brought back as well.

Even Sam got a nod that had the little eyeball scurrying for cover.

Dan didn't think he'd ever seen such a smile on Stewey's face as right now. In a way, it was almost frightening, but also reassuring.

With obvious hand gestures, Stewey had Dan and Khulan watching the archway that still seemed solid. Sam got turned around to cover the rear, just in case.

Dan glanced over his shoulder as he felt a wind rise, where none should be possible.

Stewey was glowing. Dan blinked with realization at what the man was doing. Pulling power out of the chaos around them. Just like Dan had done.

Did I glow like that? Awesome.

Stewey was wreathed in a pink flame right now, licking against what must be the silence Khulan had cast earlier. He clenched his fists and bowed his head.

Dan turned to watch forward, knowing that something big was about to happen.

Like Dan had done, Stewey apparently grounded his magic into the stones of the floor.

But where he had painted them a map with his divination, Stewey was Enchanting.

No, UnEnchanting.

Breaking.

The rim of the archway suddenly lit up with pink fire, runes glowing so hot that Dan thought they might melt their way out.

Like a soap bubble, the barrier popped, releasing a rich, sneezy batch of brimstone, but a breeze came up over his shoulders and pushed it into the room.

"Knock, knock," Stewey called out to the darkness.

NINETEEN

Man, that felt good.

Stewey had never imagined that there was that much power in existence to ground into something. Or something he could do with it. Shit, you could forge Excalibur standing in this place.

He could. Stewey had no idea what other warlocks would dream of.

Of course, they were all Conjurers and Sorcerers, weren't they? Looked down their noses at Diviners as mere Mediums, and especially Enchanters as craftsmen who should use the side entrance.

Fuckers.

He'd watched Dan. Saw how it was done. Even reached out and tasted the raw essence of the universe around them.

Heady, dangerous stuff. Man could get utterly stone-cold drunk if he wasn't careful.

Like a good Enchanter wasn't prepared.

The door shattered like an egg. Sulfur came out where

it was rotten, but Stewey was inside a construct. Everything here was an enchantment, when you got down to it. Just done by a Conjurer who probably thought he was a god or something,

Stewey had a few things to teach that bastard. And had learned divination from an expert born on the wrong side of the tracks. The kid everyone thought was just another pretty face.

Dumb-asses.

"Knock, knock."

Stewey pushed the rest of that tidal wave of power into the room, like one of those seventies disaster movies his dad liked to watch. The ones that gave you the wrong impression of how much quicksand you were likely to run into as a grown-up.

She tried to flee at the last moment, suddenly pivoting from supremacy to cowardice when somebody blew her last trap apart.

Demons were like that.

Stewey was angry.

Rage Incarnate.

And he had a firehose handy.

The laughter coming out of his mouth was probably inappropriate, but what the hell. He almost felt like a level monster from one of those computer games he'd played before he found an even more interesting imaginary world to explore with Cole Battersby.

And that pretty-boy kid from the wrong side of the tracks who turned out to be the best friend a guy could ever ask for.

Stewey flooded the room with power. Touched her, just as she was about to exit from a different archway.

No.

The opposite of chaos is not order.

It is *Pattern.*

Stewey found a pattern he liked. Grounded it hard, because that much power had to be controlled and used before he accidentally blew walls out and opened the boundaries around them.

So, he made his dreams stone.

That's what Enchanters do. The rest of you just dance around the edges, while we form the universe under your feet.

Stewey let go of the firehose and managed to stop laughing.

The little eyeball demon wasn't convinced, but he was probably more perceptive than the other two, anyway.

Stewey winked at him.

"It's safe," Stewey said, as he returned to being a mere mortal.

Gods, that could be addictive. And fun.

Both Dan and Khulan had disbelief, so Stewey set his safety and slung the shotgun by the strap. There was nothing left in that room anymore that was a threat.

Stewey entered the room and beheld the unbelievably rude thing he had done.

He really didn't like gold-diggers, demonic or not.

Caught her turning to flee, faced the wrong way, so he had to walk all the way around to where her eyes could see him. Behind him, the leftover traces of the power he had unleashed let him know when the others crossed the threshold.

"Shit, man," Dan muttered as he saw.

The chain maiden really did look like an attractive woman. Dusky and tall, like maybe she was Lebanese or Syrian. Full head of black hair. Great figure. Lovely skin.

It was the horns twisting back from her forehead like a ram's that gave her away. And the glowing red eyeballs. The tail with the arrowhead spike on the end was almost an afterthought.

She wore a simple shift he guessed was linen. Stewey knew he could unravel everything there was about the situation to *Know*, but he didn't care.

Chains emerged from her belt, the collar around her neck, and both wrists. Killing chains.

But she was no longer a threat.

Stewey had encased her a foot thick in a solid pillar of amber.

Pattern.

Organic, too, so it would preserve her and resist the sorts of magic a lady like her might manage, given a few centuries of patience.

Could a demon go insane?

Sounded like a lovely experiment.

Khulan-the-goddess walked up and tapped the amber with the hand that had been holding a powerful blur before. Even Stewey wasn't sure what would happen if that sword got too close, since it and the woman inside were kissing cousins.

She turned to him, and Stewey stopped smirking at the fly in his spider's web.

"You shouldn't be able to do that," she said simply.

Stewey smiled and asked her the one question Cole had liked to torture them with, back when they were beginner warlocks pretending to be history majors.

"What are the limits of magic?" he asked in a bright, innocent tone.

She looked at the thing he had done again, and Stewey watched all her calculations reset. Like maybe he and Dan were more dangerous than she had given them credit for.

Certainly, they were *here*, but when you were surrounded by this much power it was hard not to be. Back in the real world, she'd be head and shoulders above them, although Stewey had learned a few things in here, and Dan had as well, so maybe they were chipping away at her lead.

Stewey smiled.

"Anger is a powerful amplifier," he said in a more serious tone. "And it worked."

"It did," she agreed. "And it can be terribly seductive."

"I've seen that movie," he assured her, watching the reference to the most famous SciFi trilogy in cinematic history go right over the woman's head. "We're here. Now what?"

She looked around, almost in disbelief. Dan, too.

Stewey just smiled, but he had already tasted everything in here.

Seductive, indeed.

She still held the sword, that solid hunk of ebony darkness that was alive in ways a mundane couldn't even begin to fathom. Stewey really didn't understand the sorts of Conjuration necessary to pull that off, but he'd never been one to talk to the things that lurked just outside his barriers.

Better to Enchant things into place to keep them at bay.

Like now.

"You sane again?" Dan asked, stepping close.

Stewey bit back the response before it emerged. Maybe the laughter had held a little too much of an evil Emperor.

"Close enough for government work," Stewey grinned.

Dan smiled back, and Stewey relaxed.

Even the little eyeball, Sam, dared come closer. But he was a creature of chaos. He was way closer to what Stewey had done.

"So, this is the core?" the goddess babe asked them, looking around and walking a narrow circle.

The labyrinth was huge, when you got right down to it. Dan had mentioned something like a mile on a side. Thankfully, just a level tall, but he could see building a freaking dungeon, if you got bored enough. Layers of craziness carved out of the chaos and cast into pattern.

Maybe even raise a dragon, if you wanted to be rude.

How many of the ancients were just leftover play-things from whatever true gods existed?

Stewey had never given those legends much credence. But he'd never had access to this sort of power before. Nobody alive had.

Khulan turned and smiled at him, as if she could read his mind.

Okay, at least one. Maybe two, depending on this Koschei punk.

This was not the Thursday I had planned.

The central plaza wasn't huge or anything, looking around. The same bricks as the tunnels but faced up in rough gold. Because why the hell not?

Several lounging couches for a demoness with a lunch date to rest. Or wait like a spider at the center of her web for the next fly to land.

That's what this thing was, thinking about it. A giant spider web.

And spider babe was stuck in her own cocoon over there.

The total diameter was probably fifty yards. Waste of space, but nothing when you weren't limited by physics. The ceiling was the same fussy crap as the tunnels but pulled up into a dome that almost made the place livable, save for the medieval oil lamps lighting everything.

Stewey would have just done a lightbar all the way around and called it good. But he supposed that this Faucher punk might have been born so long ago that electricity and indoor plumbing were still novel concepts.

Dan was looking at something, moving that direction, so Stewey followed the goddess.

There was a wall hanging. Old Norman style tapestry. Or maybe the kind of quilt Dan's grandma would have made. Yeah, quilt.

Rectangle of cloth hanging from the wall, maybe three yards tall and two wide. Weird script all the way around the outside in three-inch letters. Stewey didn't understand it immediately, but it had a kind of Sanskrit feel. Not as flowy as Arabic, but not ideograms.

Pretty, though. Off-white base with yellow letters, like

drawing a spell on your white bread with the mustard bottle. Not that he'd ever done that. Never.

Historical figure with a sword and armor fighting a chain maiden.

Well, losing. Both legs trapped, plus the shield. Sword arm about to go south and make that poor bastard the next fly.

Didn't feel right, but Stewey wasn't as close as Dan or the Goddess were and didn't feel like stepping between them.

Dan was the sensor, after all. Best Diviner Stewey knew. Saw things, heard things that other folk missed, even Cole and Iliana.

Dan wasn't touching the cloth, which made sense, since it had been brought here, rather than formed. Stewey could tell that just from the way it glowed differently when he squinted.

Real world thing.

Something touched his leg, and Stewey nearly screamed as he jumped sideways, pulled the shotgun down, and had it aimed, almost before he landed.

Sam was down on the ground, arms over his head like he was expecting to get shot before Stewey processed what had happened.

Eyeball. Tugging on his pant leg to get his attention.

Yeah, worked.

"Sorry," Stewey offered, setting the safety again and pointing the gun at the ceiling.

Sam unfolded himself slowly, like a dog still expecting a kick, and Stewey felt like the worst of any two possible evils.

Dan and the Goddess had reacted to Stewey's scream. Both had blurs up. Plus one black sword.

"What is it?" Dan asked the little eyeball.

Sam blinked and drew a breath. Or something. That's what it looked like.

He turned and pointed back at the door and his eyeball got big.

Which was just weird.

Like any of this was normal.

Dan closed his own eyes, like he was communing with the dude. Cast a spell a moment later, a puff of golden smoke that raced out the door almost too fast to track.

"We've got trouble," Dan said a moment later.

"What is it?" the Goddess asked in a hard, ancient voice that kinda had Stewey wondering if she was proof against silver shot.

"Something just entered the maze behind us," Dan grimaced.

CHAPTER

TWENTY

an could feel the footsteps on the stone of the maze, following the path he had cast into the floor earlier. He wasn't sure who was making them, without throwing something large out there that might give away more than it should about what was happening here.

Certainly, it would warn whoever that they had been detected. Of course, the lady in the golden teardrop over there would have known, most likely. She'd found them quick enough.

And but for Stewey's reaction to pretty women throwing themselves at you, he'd be dead right now.

He turned and studied the chain maiden, trapped by whatever the hell Stewey had done. Walked over and studied her face where she could see him.

The eyes blinked in a comical mix of rage and terror.

He could erase the pathway, easily enough, but again, that would warn the intruder that something had noticed him.

Was the person arrogant enough to walk right along

the yellow brick road, looking for a wizard or a witch? Right now they were. He could hear footsteps in his head.

"Do we fight or hide?" Stewey asked.

Not the thing Dan had expected, but whoever was coming was probably up in those dangerous big leagues with Khulan. And probably more prepared for this situation than they had been, throwing it together on the fly.

Dan had been studying the tapestry when Sam caused all the mayhem. The intruder would be a while getting here, unless he chose to fly like the little roadrunner had, and Dan knew he would sense that.

All the pieces were there, but he didn't have them laid out on the table yet. And not much time.

Dan returned his attention to the cloth. Writing around the edges suggested a binding of some sort, but he didn't know the language. Chain maiden, on the verge of killing a crusader, from the style of armor and the device on the shield. *Ye Olde Red Cross Fleury*.

It didn't belong here. The cloth was alien.

Everything else in here, including the demon, was part of the pattern of the place, as Stewey would say. The cloth was not.

It had been brought from the outside.

With a nasty-ass guardian protecting it, after someone had already gotten through three or five layers of magical defenses, just to open the portal to this demiplane in the first place.

Valuable to Faucher, who was supposedly an ass-thumpingly powerful warlock of some sort. Who was legally dead, regardless of actuality.

Still made this activitu tomb robbing, whatever he did.

But the dead guy had no claim. Will had left things to museums, and he sure as hell wasn't bound up inside one of the Grimsbys, like the Baba Yaga supposedly was inside Khulan Zima.

Dan studied the cloth. Stewey would be figuring out how it had been enchanted. Khulan probably knew the tale being represented.

But the Diviner wanted to know why it had been brought here. And left when the guy went dead.

If he was.

Dan cast a spell at the surface of the cloth, trying to find the key to it. He wasn't even sure what he was looking for, but something just wasn't right.

"How long to engagement?" Stewey asked from about a mile away.

Dan paused to listen.

"At least thirty minutes at his current pace," Dan said. "Sam, warn us if he speeds up, please?"

He didn't bother to look but sensed the little eyeball demon's nod. Felt him move to the archway and take up a serious pose. Like the world's weirdest, tiniest gargoyle on a roof.

Dan turned his head a little to look almost side-eye at the tapestry.

"What do you see?" Khulan asked, standing close.

"Wrongness," Dan answered, unable to put it into better words than that. "He brought the tapestry here to hide it, but it's not that valuable, as near as I can tell."

"Is it hiding something?" she stepped to one side. "Like a safe in a wall?"

Click.

Dan almost felt the tumblers fall into place in his mind.

It wasn't hiding a wall safe.

It was one.

He stepped forward until he was almost touching it with his nose.

There.

Dan listened with the last traces of magic he'd held from earlier, unwilling to take the time to draw more. Or the chance that whoever was coming would sense him doing it and maybe know a way to block it.

Or do something nasty.

Dan reached out a hand. Pressed it against the knight's sword where the magic of the tapestry had an odd discontinuity.

His hand entered another pocket.

You weren't supposed to be able to do that. Put one demiplane into a second. Even the few rules chaos was willing to admit to said that they would negatively react, like Mentos and Diet Coke, and blow everything up.

Somehow, Faucher had done it.

No, this was much older. Someone else had formed the tapestry. Faucher had brought the entire demiplane into existence around it without touching.

Serious Conjurational magic there. Like maybe there had been five folks at the top level: Faucher, Khulan, Koschei, and two others whose names had been etched into that doorframe.

Dan's hand closed on something solid in the second pocket. Wrapped around it like a handle.

He drew it out, back into the room where he and the others lived.

Oh. Shit.

Sword. In a jeweled scabbard.

Not a type he recognized off the top of his head, except that it wasn't a classical longsword, nor was it a katana.

Straight, but the same width and thickness all the way down. Handle like a saber, designed to cut one way, rather than either.

Beside him, he heard Khulan's gasp.

Dan stepped back from the tapestry and saw that the knight in the picture was holding a blade very similar. Heavy cutlass, maybe, except again straight.

It didn't feel evil. Not like most of the room and labyrinth around him.

Neutral. But vibrating with power.

Serious amounts of puissance.

Dan cast a small Knowing over the whole thing. Just enough to confirm that while it might not be Excalibur, they were neighbors. Maybe cousins.

"Recognize it?" he asked Khulan and Stewey.

"No," she said shakily.

"Nyet, gospodin," Stewey said, like he did occasionally. "Might be in lust, though."

Dan pulled on the scabbard with one hand and drew the blade about twelve inches into the clear.

It glowed. Felt lovely in his hand.

Didn't say anything, which was good. He'd been afraid of finding another demon, like the thing Khulan was holding.

He looked over.

Her blade had stopped murmuring. Had gone dead quiet.

Dan slid the blade home and studied the scabbard. It also had a magical feel to it, like someone had made the two as a joint set.

Just to see if it would work, he rested it against his left hip, about where it would hang if he had the right belt.

It stuck. Hung like it was supposed to do.

Crap.

He studied the rest of the tapestry. It had to have more magic bound into it. More tricks.

But they didn't have time to explore it.

Dan muttered a little prayer to himself and grabbed the cloth, pulling hard by leaning back.

"Won't work," Stewey said a moment later. "Bound to the wall."

"Can you break it?" Dan asked. "Decided I need a new quilt in the living room when I watch television."

"Are you insane, Dan?" Khulan turned to him. "A quilt?"

"It was a joke," Dan assured her. "Don't want to leave this for our friend."

"Oh," she lapsed into silence.

Hadn't spent enough time around them to get some of the jokes, but that wasn't surprising.

He'd known Stewey for a decade.

"Hang on," Stewey said.

He did *something*, and the cloth was suddenly floating free in his hands. Dan folded it up and tossed the bundle over his shoulder.

"Sam, we still good?"

He turned to his other sidekick and got a thumbs up.

"He's coming up the path I marked," Dan explained to Khulan and Stewey. "I think we should hide from him. Not hard to do. Then sneak out when he's at the door when he gets here."

"Disrupt the path when we leave," Stewey grinned. "Make him find his way out the hard way."

"Can you undo what you did, Ogden?" Khulan asked, walking over to the new art installation by the other archway. "Release her?"

"Why the hell would I want to do that?" Stewey demanded grumpily.

"We'll be outside," Khulan smiled. "Whoever will be in here with her, without a clear route. With an angry demon. Alone."

"You are a truly evil woman, madam." Stewey grinned. "I like it."

Dan watched him concentrate for a second.

"Should be able to do it from just inside that last door," he finally said. "It will be bloody obvious, though, so you should kill the breadcrumbs at the same time. Then we hop backwards and get gone."

"Risky," Dan said, judging the options.

"Sam and I will guard the two of you while you work," Khulan said.

Dan blinked in surprise but got another thumbs up.

And she had a demon sword.

Plus he had *something* rude. Dan knew he'd have to actually draw it to be able to divine its powers, but the nature of a *demonslayer* was obvious.

"All right," Dan decided, somehow in charge here. "Sam, find us a path using the second archway. Once you do, we'll follow you out. Our friend hasn't sped up, so we've got time."

Sam nodded and took off like a roadrunner. Seriously, just like in the cartoons, where he left dust trails into and out of every single corridor, almost simultaneously.

But that was exactly what Dan had formed him for.

Less than a minute passed and Sam was back.

Grinning ear to ear, if he actually had ears.

"Let's go," Dan said, nodding to the others and taking up point.

Something was stalking them, but he had friends. They could do this.

TWENTY-ONE

Khulan wasn't sure what the hell Faucher had done. Or how. Or even why.

But the man had been concealing far more power than anyone had imagined, her included.

Dan and Stewey didn't appreciate it, but the things they had done in this demiplane were what power used to be like, three thousand years ago. Not many people would be able to appreciate it, given the timelines.

She hated to think of them as mayflies, but the goddess part of Khulan had been alive for five thousand years. She remembered the rise of iron technology, roughly the same time as the Hellenes were sacking Ilium that most famous time.

She remembered the European Dark Ages, only in that trade into the Siberian Reaches had been rich and well-developed, before collapsing, a pattern that had repeated itself any number of times since then.

She missed truly being a goddess on earth, rather than

just allowing one to ride her body for a time, until this flesh aged and another child would be chosen.

Always children. Better to find one with potential and offer her the power and immortality when young, so that the goddess might know a century in a single body, rather than having to hop constantly.

"Let's go," Dan said, nodding to them and moving towards the door, preparing to leave.

"Wait," Khulan said. "I want to check one last thing."

She didn't know why, but something about the demon had drawn her eye.

Khulan moved to face the creature again, marveling at how Stewey had been able to do something with power that she hadn't imagined possible.

But this demiplane was a dreamland. Almost anything could be done.

What were the limits to magic?

She could do things neither Dan nor Stewey could, because she used to have this much power at her fingertips every day, and not just now.

Quickly, she reached out, just as they had done, and pulled a massive amount of power to her. However, instead of casting it in one tremendous burst, she wrapped it into that fog that seemed so prevalent, the sky above every corridor.

Whoever was coming would notice it. Would react defensively.

That was fine. She wanted them twitchy. Wanted them fighting back and keyed up to do magical violence.

And she wanted to leave a signature on the invitation.

It felt like Koschei, but at the same time it wasn't. One

of his retainers, probably, sent ahead to scout. She didn't think even a deathless magic-worker would plunge as blindly into this situation as she and the men had done, however accidentally.

Would the Immortal be waiting outside the portal? Or would he still be off in his lair, carefully hidden and watching, expecting a trap?

Khulan left her flavor in the very air as she twisted the fog. Perfume, pushed into every corridor and room of this place, so the intruder would know it was her.

Would be expecting her. Koschei knew something had happened here. Every magic-worker of sufficient power on the planet had felt Dan Holt break the stepping disk, even if they didn't recognize it at the time.

Koschei would have been able to track her at least as far as Seattle. From there, it didn't take much intuition to understand that Stewey breaking down the front door of the mansion was probably her as well.

How badly do you want this confrontation, Deathless One? Enough to come through an unknown portal onto a demiplane formed by one of your competitors?

No, he would sacrifice a pawn first. Or more likely a bishop. Powerful enough that they might survive, but not enough to claim whatever prize they found inside there, like Dan had managed.

Khulan had her doubts about letting those men keep an artifact with that much power, but that was a problem to deal with tomorrow.

The three of them still had to escape this trap first.

Khulan felt the first magical bolt as the intruder felt

her presence in the fog. Knew that the person coming was a *him*, just from the signature.

Khulan smiled. He would waste time and energy preventing her from doing anything to him. Might even raise all the wrong spells as protective wards.

She turned to the demon now and smiled at it.

"You hunger, don't you?" Khulan asked.

Red eyes burned with rage. And hunger.

"He will be expecting the goddess," she told the creature, knowing that the amber only contained it.

The demon could still hear them plainly.

It blinked, since it could not nod while Stewey had her bound.

"Would you like to play a game on him?" Khulan asked.

"Do I want to know?" Dan Holt asked from the archway.

Khulan turned to him with a savage smile.

"Good does not mean innocent and virginal, Dan Holt," the goddess said ruthlessly.

He nodded some level of understanding. Protecting the world from evil did not mean one allowed evil to persist. One hunted it down and squashed it whenever one could.

Today was an opportunity Khulan hadn't known in almost a century. She didn't dare miss it.

Khulan turned back to the demon. Caught the creature's assent, as it had already guessed what she was about to do.

Khulan released the sword and the blur for a moment and placed both hands flat on the warm amber shell. Stepping past the barrier would be tricky, so she took her time, confident enough in Dan's pet to get them safely away.

She pushed all of that magical energy past the amber, letting it engulf the chain maiden and *alter* her.

Smaller. Thinner. Petite.

Blonde.

"Oh, shit," Dan whispered.

She thought it was Dan speaking. She didn't open her eyes to check. Instead, she concentrated on the binding.

If she really wanted to torture all the fool warlocks in the world, it would be so much better to shape the very flesh of the creature and bind it that way.

She left the horns, just because she knew at least one of her foes would be even more aroused by that image than just a slim, Siberian blonde woman.

"Lady, you're as bug-nuts as he is," Stewey opined as she opened her eyes.

The chain maiden had changed. Shrunk. Now she looked just like Khulan Munkhtsetseg Zima, while retaining all the chains she had before. And all the magic of such a deadly siren.

She just looked like a goddess.

"Now, we can go," Khulan smiled at her companions.

TWENTY-TWO

Dan managed to breathe again. That was frightening, what Khulan had just done. Dangerous, too, since the chain maiden would look just like her, if it ever managed to somehow get loose and walk the physical realms.

But, man, would the guy coming after them be in for a rude shock.

"Sam, you're on point," Dan said to his sidekick. "Get us out."

Sam nodded and sauntered out the archway, looking like he really wanted to light the afterburners and race. Something about getting rubber in all twelve gears.

Dan followed, making sure that the others were close. Stewey ended up in the middle, rather than Khulan, but he supposed that the sword on his hip would work quite well with the blur he spun up, in case they managed to take a wrong turn and end up facing trouble.

Near as he could tell, there were only two other people

in the labyrinth, and hopefully they'd end up meeting shortly.

And eating each other, too.

"Sam, little faster, I think," he told the spirit, picking up his own pace.

He could still hear the echo of the footsteps in his mind, but the intruder had slowed down considerably now. The man was expecting everything to be a trap and was spending time and effort trying to banish the fog that smelled just like the woman behind him.

She had a nice smell. Roses and lavender, with a hint of rain at sunrise, but he supposed that Koschei or one of the others probably wouldn't appreciate that.

It would buy him and the others time though, especially since Sam was able to navigate without putting a foot wrong. Or whatever he had.

Quickly, they moved.

One downside, the intruder had almost stopped moving, so he was barely past halfway to the central plaza of the labyrinth, rather than just about to enter it. They wouldn't have much time when they got to the portal doors, and Dan had something he wanted to try, while he still had all this power.

Tomorrow would be like waking up hung over after his twenty-first birthday party, where everything hurt, nothing worked right, and it had felt like gnomes were trying to burrow out his ears.

Sam turned a corner and suddenly they were there. Dan looked around and realized just how much of that first chamber inside had been an illusionary trap. He had been expecting a corridor at the time, so it had given him one. Had he been expecting a three-way option, there actually was one present, but it hid itself until you made your first choice.

Man, that dude was a bastard. Good thing he was dead. Hopefully dead.

Dan approached the great vault door designed to keep chain maidens inside. Sniffed at the portal and saw where someone had added a couple of new enchantments since they came through.

Probably intended to keep anyone else from opening the door and escaping while he still walked the labyrinth.

"Stewey, this one's up your alley," Dan said after a moment's inspection, moving off to one side and watching the rear with Khulan and Sam.

The urge to draw that sword was a little extreme, but he contained it for now. Might change his mind if the bad guy came barreling around the corner.

"As soon as I touch this, he's going to know," Stewey said after a moment of study. "I can break it, but he'll come a-running."

"Save it for last," Khulan said, turning to face him now. "Dan, undo the pathway first. Stewey, release your friend from her cocoon at the same time."

"He'll know it's a trap," Stewey observed neutrally.

"He knows already," she smiled rudely. "Just not what kind. Plus, if he's dealing with us, she might be able to get close to him."

Dan shuddered. Nobody should have to face something like her, but he really couldn't find a lot of sympathy in his soul for whoever had sent a shadow servant after him yesterday. Today. Eight hours ago?

Crap, all this in eight hours? I need a nap. Good thing Stewey liked to drive.

Dan turned to Sam.

"You got guard duty right now, buddy," he said.

Sam the Gargoyle nodded and *got serious.*

Dan knelt so he could actually touch the golden path he had painted on the stone with Sam's help. Unraveling it would be easy, but he had a better idea.

Again, something he wouldn't be able to do once he got outside, so why not try it now?

Dan pulsed a spell down the entire length of the path. He was already touching it in all places, that was how he'd followed the footsteps.

Now he caused the whole thing to boil off, like dry ice suddenly sublimating into a fine, golden mist.

Must have done something right. Just before it faded, he felt the intruder blast the floor. Probably thought that the mist was an attack he needed to defeat or destroy.

Hope you're getting tired and jump, bubba.

Beside him, Stewey felt a pocket supernova go off.

He'd been to LA, but never during one of their big earthquakes. Still, that's what it felt like as the whole demi-plane vibrated on a different pitch than it had before, wobbling almost onto its ear before settling down again.

Somewhere, a chain maiden was loose.

"Show off," Dan looked over at Stewey's superior smirk.

"The door," Khulan snapped. "Now. He comes."

Dan rose and brought his blur back into place. He felt heavy strides as an angry and maybe panicked warlock suddenly started to run this way.

Dan drew the sword almost automatically. It didn't weigh anything in his hand.

And it glowed. Just exactly the opposite of how Khulan's sword would consume light.

Funky.

Another pop that Dan assumed was Stewey breaking open the magic binding on the door itself. The very air popped as Stewey pushed the door back into the outer chamber.

"Let's move it, people," his friend called from what sounded like a hundred yards away.

"Go," Dan said to Khulan, feeling like he could eat a dragon for lunch.

She studied him for a second and then exited.

Dan could feel the other guy getting closer, so he backed up, sword still out and blur all ready to defend.

He was back through the doorway now.

"Let's go, Sam," he called.

Sam turned and sped to the doorway, but he bounced right off, a racquetball flattening and rebounding.

"I thought you realized," Khulan said as Sam sidled up slower this time and did his best Marcel Marceau impression.

"Realized what?" Dan demanded, reaching though and trying to pull Sam.

"He is a creature of raw chaos," Khulan said. "You cannot bring him outside of that realm, because of the way he was summoned. You'll have to leave him behind in there."

"That's a load of crap, lady," Dan snarled.

"Magic has rules," she said calmly.

"No," Stewey said abruptly. "It does not have rules. What the hell have we been up to for the last several hours?"

Dan watched his sidekick turn mournful, trapped outside safety as a wolf was coming.

"Screw that," Dan announced.

He was holding a killer sword and standing in the middle of a demiplane carved from pure chaos by an asshole with a lot of power.

What are the limits to magic? Cole had asked, time and again.

Rage, Stewey had answered today.

Dan could work with that.

He stepped back into the corridor.

"What are you doing, Dan?" Khulan demanded hotly.

"Rescuing my friend," he snapped at her. "Little help, Stewey?"

"Got your back," his best friend said, also stepping into the corridor and aiming his shotgun downrange.

To be a shit, Dan heard Stewey rack it once, catching the shell ejected and pushing it back in.

That put an armor-piercing round in the barrel. Followed by demon-killer shot. Not even magic will just stop that much mass and inertia, unless you see it coming.

Khulan remained outside, but that was fine. She'd be out of his way.

Sam looked like he wanted to cry.

Dan understood being left out when everyone else was having fun. He'd been picked last a few times, just to balance teams out evenly.

He didn't have to settle today.

Instead, he opened his mind to the chaos around them and snarled every bit of rage he had at the cosmos themselves.

Something answered, but Dan was pretty sure he didn't want to know what.

Or who.

But he felt power flowing into his limbs and that sword.

A fuck-ton lot of power.

Dan rested the point on the stone and concentrated on the uncut gemstone that made up the pommel. Blue and glowing.

He wrapped his mind around it. Concentrated.

Pushed.

Dan stuck his right hand out and felt the barrier between worlds turn solid for him, like it had Sam.

What are the limits of magic? Rage, certainly.

But there are other emotions.

Friendship was probably the best one. Stewey standing at his back to shoot something that was probably invulnerable, just because Dan needed him.

Sam, suddenly understanding that Dan wasn't willing to just abandon him, or even protect him from the monsters by UnSummoning him.

Dan pressed against the barrier. It didn't want to surrender.

Dan was done asking.

He pushed harder. Took all of that everything that someone had handed him and turned it into a diamond-tipped drill.

Ripped the very flesh of the universe open.

Not much.

Barely enough to put a golf ball through.

That was all he needed.

Sam chirped with excitement and clambered through like he was going out a window in a fire.

Once he popped to safety, Dan concentrated on the hole. Anything else would be able to escape through it, if he just left such a gap, and that would be wrong.

He needed to heal it.

Healing was an effect of Conjuration. You called friendly spirits to you and asked them to put their magic into fixing someone. There were many spirits like that, ghosts of all manner of things that had been even partly summoned over the millennia.

Pattern creatures, rather than chaos, busy putting things to right.

He wasn't sure who to ask for help, but someone had already given him the power, so he concentrated on undoing the hole. Healing the universe itself.

It was like working with cold taffy, but he pushed everything he had into it. Every drop of power that someone had gifted him. Everything in the sword.

Most of his soul.

It worked.

Dan collapsed to his knees and then face-planted when the barrier he had been resting against vanished.

He felt hands dragging him across the threshold. Little ones as well as big ones.

"Stewey, now," the Goddess called.

Dan was mostly a ball of gray fuzz, but he felt the moment when the door closed.

A sound he hadn't been aware of vanished, leaving the rest of the cosmos empty.

"He's almost there," Dan said, unaware of how he knew that.

"Good luck with that, punk," Stewey snarled as he did something.

"Can you stand?" Khulan yelled in his ear.

Except she wasn't yelling, just talking normally,

"I can try," he slurred.

Dan rolled over and got to his knees. Khulan offered him a hand up. Sam was trying to drag the sword across the floor.

"Here, let me," Dan said as he picked both of them up, Sam going onto his shoulder and Dan somehow able to slam the sword home in the scabbard blind on the first try.

Khulan had his arm across her shoulders, and he tried to help as she carry/walked him to the portal itself.

Something slammed into the labyrinth door hard enough to make it ring like a church bell.

Dan smiled. He had one tiny bit of magical energy left in his soul right now.

He turned and let it flood into the door from this side with a popping glow.

"Best of luck," he said.

"Come on." Khulan got him to the portal and they stepped onto the plane he had called reality yesterday.

It was like surfacing from under water.

Dan looked around and they were back in that room, with a chunk of wall stretched out on the floor. Sunlight was streaming in a southeast windows, but the room wasn't warm yet.

Stewey came into existence a moment later, turning and doing something to the portal that made it vanish from Dan's sight.

"What did you do, there at the end?" Stewey asked. "When you hit the door?"

"Made it disappear from the other side." Dan laughed. "Just an illusion, but it turned into raw wall and then spun him in place. Maybe he'll find his way out. And maybe the other Khulan will find him before he does."

"Now what?" Stewey asked.

Khulan the Goddess turned slowly in place, as though she was sniffing the air.

"We are alone, for now," she said. "I suggest we leave quickly."

Dan agreed. He had a sword on his hip and a tapestry rolled up across his shoulder.

"We can be in Seattle for lunch," Stewey said.

"I'm buying," Khulan replied, turning to study Dan. "But you will have to explain Sam to people."

Dan felt a hand grasp his earlobe. Soft, almost timid. But at the same time, containing the heart of a roadrunner.

"He's my friend," Dan replied. "That will be enough for my other friends."

Because it should.

EPILOGUE

Dan still felt like a helium balloon did the next morning, after it had lost just enough innards that it was hanging near the floor, rather than pushing at the ceiling.

He'd napped in the truck, in spite of the noise and the fact that the air conditioner had stopped putting out cold air again. It hadn't been worth complaining to Stewey again.

Not today.

Over the pass and out of Brown Washington into Green Washington. Roll the windows back up because it had started to mist. Down the highway towards the ocean.

Somewhere around North Bend, Stewey had suggested burgers, so they dropped off I-90 at Issaquah and ended up at Sunset Alehouse, which Dan still thought made the best burgers in the state.

They'd missed the lunch rush. Dan had an empty plate and a full beer in front of him.

Nobody had said much of anything for the last hour, beyond ordering and passing salt and ketchup around.

He turned to the woman next to him. She was a woman again, at least here. The Goddess, or whatever she was, had receded. Maybe she only came out on other planes of existence.

Yesterday, Dan had seriously doubted such things still existed. Too much magic lost over the centuries, so that nobody could do something like that anymore.

How much of the truth was wrapped up in a few, powerful beings, hoarding it all to themselves instead of sharing? Locking it into things like the sword hidden in plain sight on the gun rack in the parking lot with a glamour that made it invisible to mundane eyes?

Sam was guarding it for now, so the sword, the tapestry, and the truck were all safe. At least from everything but pigeons.

What was an old Ford pickup without pigeon shit somewhere?

Khulan was staring back at him with hooded eyes. Pretty, jade eyes. A thousand miles deep and older than time.

He stuck his hand out.

"Dan Holt," he said, only partly kidding. "Pleased to meet you."

She got jolted pretty hard by that, which was part of his intent. The eyes lost something. Became more human. Almost warm.

"Khulan Zima," she replied awkwardly, taking it.

Stewey got into the act, and suddenly it looked like a

pair of insurance agents selling annuities to a customer. Or something equally innocent.

"So now what?" Dan asked, picking up his lager and taking a long sip.

"I would say you two have accidentally been initiated into a war that goes back millennia, but that happened a week ago," she said. "Now, you might have made some enemies, depending on what happened to the intruder in the labyrinth."

"Do we know who he was?" Stewey asked. "Or what?"

"One of Koschei's people," she turned to the man, eyes serious again. "He left traces outside that I was able to identify."

"There was no other car in the driveway when we left," Dan pointed out.

"And there are other ways to travel," she replied, smiling just a little. "There used to be a pretty powerful stepping disk in the back yard, until a pair of vandals came along and destroyed it."

"Huns," Dan corrected her.

That was his historical specialty, more or less.

"Huns," she agreed. "I should get you proper costumes."

Dan wanted to laugh but had a moment of pure fear that she might actually have something in a trunk somewhere. All of those tribes had originated north and east of the Roman Empire, in places that would become Poland and Russia much later. The Siberians had probably traded with them.

"So now what?" Stewey steered them back to the starting point like a bloodhound after a bit of kibble.

"Now you have both stepped up your power," she said, serious again. "I saw that, even if you didn't. Not enough to challenge Koschei or one of the others, but you are more dangerous than you were a week ago. Plus, you possess items of significant power that are normally rare in the modern age, so that will make you targets of thieves and scholars."

Dan nodded. He agreed with her on both points. He'd felt something break and reshape inside himself, up in that maze. More power at his fingertips. Maybe more power that he could contain, once he had a long nap and a few days to recover.

Stewey had reached out and wrapped a chain maiden in amber. Seriously.

And then undone it, which was even more impressive.

What were the limits to magic?

"Are you really a goddess?" Dan asked, trying to square this gorgeous, petite blonde with Mongolian cheekbones, against a semi-divine being that had haunted Russian folklore for at least a thousand years.

"We have all been the Baba Yaga, Dan," she said carefully. "Khulan was just the latest of her acolytes offered the honor of hosting the goddess for her lifetime."

"Offered?" Stewey asked.

"Offered," she nodded. "I have memories that stretch beyond the dawn of recorded history, Stewey. But I am still human. A few years younger than you two in the flesh, but I will most likely outlive you by half a century before passing the torch to another."

"And Koschei the Deathless?" Dan asked.

"A collector of things," she said. "Items. He hides his soul in such items and then hides them in other things. Perhaps he carves out demiplanes and puts pockets inside them, like the tapestry you took from Faucher. There might have been an egg in there with Faucher's soul in it when you reached in. I have no idea where the sword came from and don't have access to my library to research it."

"We've got a pretty good library in Moscow," Dan said, stumbling as she did a double-take. "Moscow, Idaho. Iliana would probably kill to get a chance to meet you, because she might be a branch of your order. Or whatever it is you folks do."

"I'm not sure she should know about me, Dan," Khulan replied. "At least not yet. Koschei and others will come after you for the power you possess. That puts Cole and Iliana at risk."

"All the more reason to warn them," Dan countered. "Plus, you either have a copy of the book and need to read her translation or need to make a copy of it."

"We'll see," she said quietly. "You two still represent wild cards suddenly thrust onto a gaming board so old that it would frighten you."

"So how do we make the world a better place?" Dan asked. "And how do we bring back magic to the world? I got a feeling that we need it."

"It's not as easy as destroying that demiplane," she said. "That would just unravel the chaos. You'll need to bring the power up from the depths of the earth where it has settled and fallen asleep. And it won't necessarily want to wake."

"Okay," Dan agreed, checking with Stewey and getting a nod.

"Just like that?" she blinked in surprise.

"We're already part of your war," he said. "And you've been the exact opposite of that asshole who sent a shadow servant to tear apart our barriers. You've asked. You've helped. Not once have you demanded or even suggested that we turn all of these items over to you for safekeeping."

"Oh," she said, seemingly taken aback. "It will be risky."

"Right, because breaking a stepping disk was the smartest way to handle the situation," Dan laughed.

"Plus, what about Sam?" Her eyes bored in on him.

"He's currently into the AC system, trying to figure out where you've got a coolant leak." Dan laughed.

"He's what?" Stewey popped up and almost stood.

"He's not touching anything, Stewey," Dan reassured the man. "Literally inside the vents looking for leaks. I'm guessing that most mundanes won't ever see him, will they?"

She paused for a moment and then nodded.

"Unless he stands right in front of them and waves, no," she agreed. "They'll see a flash of something from the corner of their eye and dismiss it. Warlocks and magic-workers will know him for what he is."

"What he is is a magical goofball with a speed fetish," Dan said. "And my friend."

"Yes." She nodded to both of them. "I would be your friend as well, if you would have me."

Dan smiled.

"So now we're pawns in the War for Eternity?" he asked.

She laughed.

"Pawns could not do what you gentlemen have already done," she said. "But it will get harder."

"That's fine," Dan said. "I've got a lot of friends I can call on."

READ MORE

To read more of my fiction, sign up for my newsletter. You'll also get a free book!

http://www.blazeward.com/newsletter/

ABOUT THE AUTHOR

Blaze Ward writes science fiction in the Alexandria Station universe (Jessica Keller, The Science Officer, The Story Road, etc.) as well as several other science fiction universes, such as Star Dragon, the Dominion, and more. He also writes odd bits of high fantasy with swords and orcs. In addition, he is the Editor and Publisher of *Boundary Shock Quarterly Magazine*. You can find out more at his website www.blazeward.com, as well as Facebook, Goodreads, and other places.

Blaze's works are available as ebooks, paper, and audio, and can be found at a variety of online vendors. His newsletter comes out regularly, and you can also follow his blog on his website. He really enjoys interacting with fans, and looks forward to any and all questions—even ones about his books!

Never miss a release!

If you'd like to be notified of new releases, sign up for my newsletter.

http://www.blazeward.com/newsletter/

Buy More!

Did you know that you can buy directly from the KRP website?

https://www.knottedroadpress.com/shop/

Connect with Blaze!

Web: www.blazeward.com
Boundary Shock Quarterly (BSQ):
https://www.boundaryshockquarterly.com/

ABOUT KNOTTED ROAD PRESS

Knotted Road Press publishes dynamic fiction set in exotic locations and unique non-fiction voices in genres such as autobiography, business, cookbooks, and how-to. Our authors cover a wide range of genres including science fiction, fantasy, mystery, literary, and poetry, appealing to all readers. We offer both DRM-free ebooks and print books for a global readership.

Knotted Road Press
www.KnottedRoadPress.com
www.KnottedRoadPress.com/Shop